See How She Falls

Book Three:
The Chronicles of Izzy

Michelle Graves

Dedication

For Susan Pszczolkowski Baxter.
May your eternal garden be filled with cozy reading
nooks and brilliant stories.
You are missed.

Acknowledgments

To my husband, the innovator of bad guys, and brilliant story-teller in his own right. My books would be impossible without his love, patience, and advice. Even if I never take it. I love you more than you will ever, ever know!

Wendy, I shall never be able to convey how much I love you. Fate certainly brought you into my life, and I can honestly say, you take my breath away. (See what I did there?) In all seriousness, my books would never be as amazing without all of your guidance, support, honesty, and help. You are more important to me than you can even imagine!

Ali, you are just, well, there aren't enough words. I am so blessed to not only call you friend, but to have you be a part of my writing process. I know that I can always count on you for honesty, support, and angry messages. Your enthusiasm for Izzy keeps me motivated!

Charissa and Shawn, for some reason when I think of one of you, I think of the other. The two of you are like the book sisters I never knew I could have. I am so blessed that the past year and these books have brought us closer together. What started with books has led to two beautiful and everlasting friendships. I love you both BIG, HUGE even!

Regina, even when life gets super busy, just know that I love you and I am so thankful that you keep on reading. Even if you will never love Aberto. (But you will, someday!)

Dianne, you mean the world to me. I love you to bits and it is more than just the help you so willingly give me, it is your optimism. It is downright contagious. I never have to worry about a thing with you. I know you will be honest and loving and gentle

To my new sisters at Dauntless Indies, thank you so much for all of the advice, the help, and the guidance you have given a newbie like me. You are three of the most amazing women I've ever known!

Syd Gill, you are a saint! No seriously, you are so amazing. There aren't enough good things I can say about what you do for The Chronicles of Izzy. The book covers are brilliant and I know without a doubt, you will always come through for me! You, my dear, are one talented genius!

Neeley Bratcher, I want you to know how much I appreciate you taking the time to give my books the love they deserve. Even with all you have going, working full time and writing your own brilliant books, you still take the time for me.... It means more than you can know! I love you to bits!

Michelle's Mafia, you people are the best Street Team, support, friends a girl could ever ask for! Thank you for all of your hard work and pimping. I'd be nothing without all of you! Love you to bits!

And to you, the person that picked up The Chronicles of Izzy and have stayed with me, thank you. You mean, well the world to me! Without you, this would just be a computer file hanging out in my laptop. The enthusiasm and excitement of each of you has propelled me to keep on doing this! So thank you for taking a chance on Runs and sticking with me!

Prologue

And so it was, the gathering of Seers, the last of the soul walkers. They came together to bind the future so that the darkness may never prevail. Their pleas went out to the gods both old and new, to the Guardians that they may raise themselves up to protect the one to come, and to the Old Ones to anoint her path.

The cries went up to the heavens and the heavens heard. An oath was made from the gods to the keepers of man. There would be a Seer when time came to pass. A Seer unlike any other before or after. The assurance of the gods echoed with an oath to the soul walkers that there would be signs.

There would be signs anointing the Seer's path so that she may be known to those that knew to look. The Seer to come shall be the last of the soul walkers, but the first of her kind. She will traverse the planes, both in present and past. Her powers will manifest tenfold and her path shall be anointed so that she may fight the darkness.

And while the promise of the one to come brought great comfort to the Seers, the last of the soul walkers, the binding of the oath left them to doubt. The gods promised to provide the Earth with a great protector, but as in all things, the protector must choose. The Seers did not understand and began to question the gods.

The gods responded, and it is their answer that set flame to the fears that the darkness may well prevail. The Seer to come must choose to face the darkness coming. Her path will be filled with turmoil and her soul marked by loss. Though she will have the strength to fight the darkness, she must be willing to surrender all.

To end the darkness, the Seer must fall.

Chapter One

It was finally time. Molly's mom had been held captive for over two months while we tried to pry information from her. Unfortunately, Elaine wasn't the fount of knowledge we had hoped she'd be. I looked over to where she sat, all prim and proper as though her world wasn't about to be completely upended. The lack of remorse in her eyes sickened me. No matter how hard I tried, I couldn't understand how Elaine could so dispassionately slay Seers, betray her daughter, and feel nothing akin to regret. Something in her had broken at some point. Maybe Molly had been right, maybe it had been when she lost her husband. No matter what she'd gone through, I couldn't excuse what she'd done. Not to Molly, not to the Seers, and not to me.

"Izzy, the time is upon us." Aberto's solemn voice startled me out of my reverie.

"Alright, I'm ready." I stood and walked to the center of the platform, the same one used during my protection mark ceremony only months before. I rooted myself in place, gathering my courage as I thought of the ceremony that was about to take place. Elaine would be stripped of her powers for the rest of her long life, something that wasn't to be done lightly.

"I call the Council to order." My voice echoed through the massive group. Aberto nodded his head almost imperceptibly, encouraging me to continue. "We are gathered to strip the Betrayer of her Gifts. She has forsaken all that our people hold to be true. Elaine has turned her back against her fellow Seers

3

and walked the path of darkness. For this, she shall be stripped of her powers and be banished from the Order forever. There will be no shelter from Seer nor Guardian found. From this day forward she shall be nothing more than a memory in our collective."

Aberto turned toward Elaine, leveling her with his gaze. "Do you wish to say anything before we begin?"

"You think you know what is coming. You think you know where the threat lies. Everyone here is going to die." Elaine's maniacal laughter sent chills rushing down my spine. Her words only reinforced the fears that had been building since we'd captured her months ago. "Oh, and Izzy, you can't hide forever." Looking into Elaine's eyes, I finally understood. No sanity remained there. Whomever she'd once been was there no more.

Elaine smiled at me, ready to incite more fear at any moment. In a split second, Aberto rushed toward her, wrapping his hand around her mouth violently to cut off her unsaid words. Brutally pulling her head back, he whispered in her ear, "We will hear no more, Betrayer." He leveled her with his stony gaze. I had only been on the receiving end of that look a few times. It made my knees shake just thinking about it. For a second, I almost felt sorry for Elaine. Aberto could be truly frightening when he wanted to be.

"Let us begin." Aberto tossed Elaine's head roughly to the side and moved to retrieve his tattoo implements. He pulled out a stylus and moved towards her body. Her face was an immovable mask as he approached her. Not a trace of remorse shone behind her eyes. He placed the stylus against her skin and made the first mark.

Elaine's scream tore through the crowd, sending a shockwave that reverberated against everything in its path. For a moment, I wondered if we were doing the right thing. Surely there had to be some other way to keep her from using her powers. Just as the thought danced across my mind, I remembered Ren and everyone else that had perished because of this woman's selfishly callous behavior. She deserved a far worse fate than the one she had been given. If it were up to Molly, she would already be dead.

I scanned the crowd looking for Molly. Things had been in such an upheaval since this all began that I'd hardly had any time to spend with her. I wanted more than anything to be by her side right now. But, I had a place. I was the leader of the Council now and that meant I was not at the liberty to follow my own whims any longer, a lesson I'd learned the hard way only weeks before. My life no longer belonged to me. Molly sent a sad smile in my direction and turned her attention back to where her mother sat, still screaming bloody murder. Someone should shove a sock down the woman's throat. I was getting sick of hearing her yelps.

I watched Aberto as he moved around her marking her so that she would be unable to use her powers. He muttered words both foreign and familiar as he carved into her skin. These marks were not the beautiful ones he had bestowed upon my body. They were crude lines that gouged into her skin so deeply there was no doubting their permanence. He looked up to catch my eyes momentarily before turning back to his work.

The look in his eyes in that moment spoke volumes. Ever since he'd life breathed me, or whatever the hell he'd done, we shared a weird connection. I was always cognizant of his presence and whenever we were near one another, I found myself drawn closer to him. I rationalized that it was

5

just the part of his spirit living within me that called to him. Yep, that was it. His soul inside of me longed to be back with its other half. That was my story, and I was sticking to it.

"NOOOOOOOOO!" Elaine's scream snapped me back to the present, just as another shockwave ripped through the gathered Council members, Seers and Guardians. An audible snap sounded that left no doubt about what had just happened. Elaine's powers were gone.

"Just kill me," she whimpered.

I saw Molly start toward the stage. She'd been trying to kill her mom ever since Ian had brought her back from the old factory. Before she even made it a step from her seat, Ian pulled her back and whispered something in her ear. She sat rigid in her seat clenching and unclenching her fists. I drew her attention and shook my head slightly. I wouldn't have her doing something that she would regret the rest of her life. No matter how mad she was at the woman, she was still her mother.

"Elaine, you will find no refuge from our kind from this day forward. You will live the rest of your very long life alone in the world of humanity. Perhaps, in this new life you will find some way to atone for your betrayal." Aberto leaned close to her ear and whispered the rest. "May your judgment be merciless. May the rest of your days upon this earth be a torment, for you deserve no less."

With that, Aberto poofed. I still didn't really know how he did it. One second he was there, then the next, gone. He would make an excellent magician. Perhaps we could raise money for the Council that way. "The Amazing Aberto." It could work. It would be an excellent Vegas show. I shook myself from my thoughts and looked back at the crowd. Time to be the leader.

"The Division will remove Elaine from the grounds. They will place her in a suitable home, far from here. No one shall seek her out, none shall provide her with comfort. If anyone is found disobeying this directive, they will also be stripped of their abilities. We have been called to a higher purpose. We are meant to provide stability in a world that is lost to chaos. While it may seem more appealing to use our gifts in a way that will bring us fame or fortune that is not what we were made to do. Our lives are meant to be lives of service and sacrifice. If you feel you are not up to fulfilling this task, I am sure the Old One can return and strip you of your powers as well. A darkness is coming people, and we must pull ourselves together and fight. There will be no refuge for traitors within this Council." I eyed everyone in the crowd steadily, I wanted to see if there was a weak link that I'd missed. I was truly tired of being blindsided.

The gathered crowd stared back at me. Their expressions were part horror, part pride. Two months ago I would have balked at the responsibility that now rested upon my shoulders. Now, I would be damned if I let anyone else be hurt. I'd grown tired of losing everyone I held dear; of watching people die and being powerless to stop it. Enough was enough, and I was determined to put an end to whatever darkness was coming. No matter what the cost may be.

"It is finished, you are free to go." I watched as they moved back toward the house. Only the four Council members remained. The last four people I wanted anywhere near me at the moment.

I'd been doing my durndest to hide the changes that were happening within me. It had started with my eyes. Right after Aberto had breathed part of his soul into me, my eyes became this churning miasma of blue and hazel. They never quite settled on one color or another. Luckily, only the people I truly trusted had seen them before I started to wear contacts. It wasn't exactly a natural thing I was experiencing. In fact, I was the first person that had ever been saved by an Old One. No one really knew what was going to happen to me. Each day, things changed a little bit more, and never at a time that would be convenient. Like yesterday, I accidentally eavesdropped on Ian as he mentally undressed Molly. Not something I wanted to ever see again, that's for sure.

"Milady, we have some questions if you are at the leisure to answer them," one of the Council members said, I think her name was Damali. Her skin was a beautiful, dark tan denoting her Arabic descent. She was utterly stunning. I still wasn't used to these people answering to me. After all, they had been around far longer than I had, and they probably expected to ascend to Council Leader when Isadora passed on.

"I have nothing else going on, would y'all like to go to the office and discuss your questions? I think it might be more comfortable." As the words left my mouth, I realized I'd just pulled an Isadora. I had posed a question that really left no room for argument. They would come, of that I was sure.

"That would be lovely," Damali's Guardian bellowed. I was convinced that the man was physically incapable of speaking at a normal decibel. Every word out of his mouth threatened to burst my ear drums. I wondered if anyone had ever told him about his voice modulation problem.

"If you would follow me." Kennan stepped forward, pulling me from my mental inquisition in the process.

As we moved toward the office I thought about my Guardian, the man I loved. Things had been, in a word, tense between us. I hated it. There was a rift between us ever since I started to change. It wasn't exactly like I could fix this. I didn't ask for Aberto to breathe his life force into me and save me. In reality, the changes just made it abundantly clear that our old life could no longer exist. It was something I'd accepted months ago. He had not.

We moved into the office and sat down to discuss whatever questions the Council had. I wasn't sure I wanted to be that close to them. Hiding my new talents, and freakish physical changes, was not exactly easy.

Chapter Two

I gazed at the faces of the Council members, all four of them, and wondered why I'd been so afraid of them last year. Before, they were an imposing force, but now they just looked like a bunch of sullen children. Of course they were paired off in their wonderful Guardian-Seer duos. I still couldn't make heads or tails of how this whole matching system worked. As far as I could tell, the two sets would have done better with switching Guardians.

Pulling myself from my musings, I found Damali sourly gazing at me. There was something completely off-putting about her that I couldn't quite explain. She had this way of making me feel like I was always wrong, even when I was right. Then, there was her Guardian, who had taken up a post, brooding behind her. I wasn't really sure what his name was, but it should be Brutus. In my mind, he was a Brutus. I imagine all men that are unable to regulate their voices should be called Brutus.

Then there was Francesca, she was just a waif of a thing. She sat there drawing imaginary circles on the floor with her toe. Francesca was downright unsettling. It was as if she was always in the future and never the present. Whatever she saw there seemed to weigh down upon her shoulders, crushing her until her frail body could not even remain upright. A fierce intelligence shone through her eyes that belied a millennia of secrets. Then, there was her Guardian, Eric. His name I knew. He was a domineering bastard, if there ever was one. Eric loved to push his way into any and every conversation just to prove how intelligent he was. All he succeeded in doing was pissing everyone off.

Feeling someone's eyes upon me, I looked up to find Kennan's gaze locked upon me. He raised a brow in my direction as if to ask me what the heck was going on. I had no idea what the Council members wanted, but I would find out.

"So, you have questions?" I ventured, to end the oppressive silence.

"We want to know how it came to be that Isadora was so carelessly taken. Why were we not called in immediately following her disappearance? We should have been informed." Damali leveled me with her gaze, making me feel like a petulant child.

"Honestly, we were so busy trying to figure out how to put an end to the insanity, we didn't have time to organize our thoughts. I was thrown into this position, and I've been playing catch up ever since. I assure you, it isn't a mistake that will happen again." I wouldn't succumb to bullying. I'd been through far too much, and knew that I had far more to come. I wasn't going to add a spoiled Council member to my list of woes.

"In the future, we would appreciate being apprised of anything that so wholly affects Seers," Brutus shouted. Seriously, I needed ear plugs around the man. It was intolerable.

"In the future, I would appreciate your support. I understand that things are tense right now. None of us expected Isadora to die. Well, none of us except for, perhaps, her. Now, we are left with a much larger problem. So, if we can put our differences behind us for the moment and deal with the problems at hand, that would be fantastic."

"What problems? We thought that Elaine had been dealt with." Francesca's soft voice broke me out of my staring contest with Brutus. I really needed to figure out what his real name was.

"I was given a warning. It is part of the reason I requested that you join us. Something is coming. The darkness shall descend and we must be prepared to fight it."

"Don't be ridiculous," Francesca murmured. "The darkness is a myth. A terrible story we tell our children to keep them in line. You are young still. Someday you will understand how things really are." She looked up momentarily, her empty eyes focusing on nothing, before she turned her attention back to the circles she was tracing with her toe.

"You may find it ridiculous, heck you may not even believe me. I get that. I'm young, I'm new at all of this, and most of all I don't know the history of our people. That doesn't mean that it isn't the truth. Ren gave me the warning, straight from the heavens themselves. When God talks, I listen." I tried my best to keep my temper in check. There was no telling what new powers might manifest if I got too upset.

"It isn't that we don't believe you, dear," Damali placated. "We just need proof."

I stared at all of them for a breath before rolling up the sleeve of my shirt. I'd kept the runes well hidden since they'd appeared, so they weren't common knowledge. As I held my arm out for closer inspection a strange look crossed their faces. It was half awe, half revolt. I couldn't make sense of it. All I did know was that I wished they'd gone away when the other Seers were freed like I thought they would.

"Is this proof enough?" I wanted to see their honest reactions. I needed to know whether I could trust them to be on my side. I wanted to believe that they would be able to help me with whatever was coming.

"When did those runes begin?" shouted Brutus.

"Around the time the Seers started disappearing. We believed the runes to be somehow connected to their deaths. Unfortunately, we were wrong," Kennan chimed in.

"Do any of you have any knowledge of what this darkness is supposed to be, or further information about the prophecy?" I needed something from them.

"Don't tell me you think you are the Seer to Come?" Eric's voice dripped with contempt.

"All signs point to yes," I deadpanned. I really hated that guy. He was such an asshat. I had my own issues to deal with. I didn't need him being all, "You aren't allowed at the cool kid's table," with me.

"What evidence do you have to support this?" Francesca asked slowly.

"My oath," Aberto chimed in, once again appearing out of thin air.

That was another fun thing that had developed. He could sense whenever I was becoming upset and would appear randomly to check on the situation. This stupid, seemingly irreversible connection between us was becoming a nuisance. It was unnerving and something that I'd been meaning to discuss with him. And from the look on Kennan's face at Aberto's sudden appearance that talk needed to happen soon.

"Old One, you have no place in this Council meeting," Eric chimed in.

"Don't forget your place, Guardian." Aberto's eyes lit up with a cold fire. "My place is anywhere the Council leader needs me. You doubt her word, you doubt her actions, and you seem to think she is friendless in our world. Do not underestimate her, or you will be found wanting."

"My apologies," Eric mumbled.

"I don't want this to turn into an argument. I'm not trying to debate whether or not I'm the Seer from the prophecy. Honestly, it would be super awesome if it weren't me. What I need from y'all is information. I need to know everything I can about the darkness, about the prophecy, about what is coming our way. The only way we are going to be able to survive this is to prepare. Do any of you have anything at all that might help?"

"All of our resources are back at our homes. Obviously, our presence here is unnecessary. We can assist you from there," Damali answered snidely.

"If you think returning to your homes is the best move, then by all means, don't let me stop you. But I'm holding you to your word. You say you can assist me from there, and there better be some assistance coming my way. If not, I can easily find a new Council. There was nothing left in Isadora's notes about retention of Council members." I raised an eyebrow, waiting for any of them to respond.

"We shall help you in any way we can, Milady." Damali's tone seemed sincere, but I didn't have the best track record in judging people's character.

"If that is all you can give me, then you are dismissed," I said, turning toward my desk. I wanted them gone. I was tired of wearing the contacts, I was tired of worrying about what new talent may develop in their presence, and most of all, I was tired of trying to fill the role of Council Leader. I was exhausted beyond belief.

"May the gods shine favorably upon you," Brutus shouted as they made their exit.

Chapter Three

I waited until I heard the door shut to look up. When I did, I found Kennan and Aberto both staring at me. I decided it was time for some answers; answers I'd been waiting on for weeks. I needed to understand what Aberto was. I'd been struggling, trying to understand what I was becoming, and I knew, without a doubt, that his secret held some of the answers I sought.

"Kennan, I need to speak with Aberto alone for a moment." I pleaded with my eyes. I knew that my request would just add to the tension brewing between us, but I could only deal with one problem at a time.

"If that is your wish." Kennan's voice came out strained through gritted teeth.

"I need answers." That was all I could give Kennan. Any more explanation, and he would once again begin to fret over my well-being. Lately, he had been either distant or smothering, never just the Kennan I was used to.

"I will wait right outside the door. Please come and get me when you are finished." Kennan left without sparing me another glance. It hurt deep in my chest that things were so off with us. I just didn't know how to make him believe that my changes didn't change how I felt about him.

"I need to know the truth," I choked out. I knew that Aberto had been keeping a lot of secrets from me, and I also knew that he said I would regret knowing the truth.

"Can we sit?" Aberto's gruff voice sounded from behind me.

"Sure." I swallowed deeply, not wanting to address the other issues at hand.

"What would you like to know?" he asked, after we had arranged ourselves in the two wingback chairs close to the fireplace.

"What are you? I only ask, because I want to understand what is happening to me. In order for me to do that, I think I need to know all that I can about you."

"Are you sure that you want the truth. It is not a pretty tale, Izzy. This is a tale of shame, of a curse that I carry with me through the rest of time. Modern Seers and Guardians have forgotten the truth. The Guardians revere Old Ones as the beginnings of their lineage. They have painted us as their guides, their source of wisdom. Which is what we have made them believe over thousands of years. The truth is far uglier. No one, aside from those cursed, knows the truth. Are you sure this a burden you wish to bear? It is a secret that I would ask not be shared with anyone, not even your Guardian."

"I need to know, Aberto. If that means I have to keep a secret, so be it. It isn't like I'm not already keeping stuff from him." I closed my eyes and pulled in a deep breath, trying to chase away my sadness. I opened my eyes slowly, trying to convey in mere seconds what could take an eternity to say. "Please, I need the truth."

"The truth." Aberto paused. "The truth may be easier to show you than to tell you. Will you come with me?" He reached his hand out to me, pleading with his eyes.

"Where?" I asked.

"I want to take you back to the beginning, the dawn of the Guardians. If you wish to know me, to truly understand what it is that I am, then you must see it for yourself."

"Okay." I reached my hand out and entwined my fingers with his. Immediately, I was ripped into the dreaming, or vision, or whatever it was. I really missed the days when I just had one or the other.

"Where are we?" I whispered, afraid my voice may draw unwanted attention.

"We are in the place where it all changed, the moment I became what you see before you now." Aberto said, pointing towards a much younger, less troubled visage of himself. *"This is the culmination of my fall. This, Izzy, is the man I used to be. The man I would still be if it weren't for the wisdom of the gods. We are on the island of Santorini."*

"Why are we here, and maybe more importantly, when are we here?" I questioned Aberto. Nothing looked remotely familiar. The beautiful buildings I associated with Santorini were nowhere to be seen.

"The year is 1645 BC, and we are here because I did not heed the warnings whispered by the gods. If I had, these people would still be alive." I turned to look at Aberto only to find a darkness staring back. *"I was arrogant, and in that arrogance, I failed them."*

"What do you mean?"

"I will show you." Aberto led me closer to his younger self. As soon as we were within earshot, he pulled me to a stop. *"Listen."*

I did as he asked. I stood rooted to the ground, my attention rapt as the scene played out before my eyes. Aberto stood talking to several men that appeared to be similar in age. Scanning the group, I counted seven, all listening intently to the words coming from Aberto.

"We must not interfere, that is the role of the Seers. If they have not given us the direction, we cannot move," Aberto declared. His voice resounded throughout the group, carrying with it a confidence that would not be refuted.

"If we do nothing, they will die. We were given the vision Aberto, are we not meant to use it?" A man asked, timidly questioning Aberto's guidance.

"If the gods wanted us to act, do you not believe they would have given us a firm resolve? Yet, here we stand, unable to decide. The gods would have guided us firmly had this been their purpose." Aberto seemed determined to sway the men away from action.

"It's as he says. Aberto's wisdom has guided us without fault thus far, we should put our faith in him that he will not lead us astray." With that the men all seemed to come to some sort of agreement. All but the one that had questioned him earlier. He seemed to doubt the wisdom in Aberto's words.

"I don't understand, you were just doing what you thought was right." I turned toward my Aberto, trying to make sense of what I had seen.

"No, I was doing what was easy. I was so confident that the gods would lay everything right at my feet. My arrogance and naivety led me to believe all of the answers would be easy. Yet, the gods had given me everything I needed to fulfill my calling. They had shown all of us the truth, and instead of trusting the gods, they put their faith in me. I led us all to destruction."

"But what happened? Are all seven of you still alive? What does it mean that this was the beginning of your fall?"

"This wasn't the only time I made such a foolish decision. The men looked to me for guidance and I led them astray more times than I can count. In my belief *that I knew exactly what my purpose was, I misdirected the men who trusted me. Now, we are all cursed."*

"Aberto, you're still talking in riddles. I'm not closer to understanding any of this than I was before."

"We should return, your Guardian may grow worried," Aberto said, taking my hand in his and pulling us back from the vision.

"Oh, you are so not out of the doghouse, mister. I want answers. Not riddles. Answers." I was doing my best not to toss my cookies all over the office rug.

"It is not an easy thing for me to tell, Izzy. It has been thousands of years since these events took place. The memories have been somewhat dissolved. I will do my best to explain everything."

"Okay, so this is what I understand so far. You and these seven dudes were Guardians and you screwed up?" I wasn't even sure they were Guardians to be honest.

"No, we were more than Guardians. We were the original Guardians. The first of our kind. We were sent from the heavens as ambassadors to protect this world from the darkness that prowls just outside of this realm. We were sent with seven Seers to help one another balance the outcome of the world. We were thrown into this world like some sort of divine experiment." Aberto gritted his teeth together in anger. "The Seers went mad before failing completely. The gods had not predicted the overwhelming affect the visions, combined with other abilities, might have on a human brain. Ultimately, through years of experimentation, the gods formed a group of Seers that could resist the madness and fulfill their duty. That is a story for another time. I told you, the memories get a bit muddled. When the Seers fell, the seven of us were asked to fulfill their duties as well. We failed."

"How so?"

"We were unable to see clearly what the Seers might see. In my arrogance, I thought I understood what the gods were saying and acted as though I had all of the answers. Sadly, I was mistaken. I led my brothers straight to their destruction. We failed more times than I can count to protect innocents from events that were never meant to be. Finally, the gods grew angry with us. With me. They cursed us to roam this realm until we pay penance for our misdeeds. I am cursed to wander here until the gods feel I have restored the balance."

"But what is the curse? Is it that you can never die? Am I going to be immortal now?" I started to hyperventilate. I'd thought three hundred years was a long time. It was nothing compared to an eternity.

"The curse is simple. We are to guide Seers and Guardians. We must help them to fulfill their purpose, yet we are never to interfere. We must guide others to maintain the balance that we so miserably failed to control. So we walk between planes, never truly belonging to either. We spend years in the fog sometimes, not even realizing the time has passed. I have lost track of most of my brothers. I know not if they have passed on; if they have been able to fulfill their calling and restore balance enough to garner the gods' forgiveness. I can only speak for myself. I was lost in my own misery, lost in the fog for centuries. You changed everything."

"And then you changed me." I sat heavily in the chair, unsure if I wanted to hear more.

"Yes, and then I changed you. I changed you, and I may very well have cursed you to an existence like my own. You may wish me to regret my choice to save you, to interfere when I was not meant to. I saw your future; you weren't supposed to die that day, Izzy. I will not now, nor shall I ever, regret the choices that I've made where you are concerned." Aberto's gaze rested on my face as though he expected some sort of thanks for what he had done.

"So, are all of you still around? I mean, the Old Ones. Are y'all just drifting around in the fog waiting for some metaphysical bell to ring and bring you back to this plane? More importantly, you never answered the immortal question."

"I don't know about my brothers, where their fates have led them. All I know is of my own existence. I am as eternal as the gods will me to be. I have no way of knowing if this curse, this existence, will be your fate as well." His face fell as he looked upon me. I knew that my chances weren't looking all that great.

"There is something else I want to know." I hesitated, unsure I was really ready to hear the answer. I breathed out just as he pulled a classic Aberto.

"Our time is up for now, Izzy. I shall return when you need me." And just like that he was gone. The son of a biscuit eating, question avoiding, pain in my arse.

Chapter Four

I got up from the chair and stretched out my tense muscles. The stress of the past months weighed heavy on me as I made my way toward the door and another talk that couldn't wait any longer. It was time that Kennan and I got to the root of our problems. There was absolutely no way I could face whatever was coming if I was constantly worried about where we stood. I needed him to be normal again, or at least treat me the way he used to.

As I rested my hand on the door knob, I inhaled slowly. This was something I couldn't avoid. I opened the door and stared out at my Guardian. He was sitting against the wall staring down at his folded hands. His brow creased with worry or anger, I wasn't sure which.

"Kennan?" my voice was barely above a whisper.

"Done so soon?" his icy response chilled me.

"We need to talk." I finally found my voice. I wouldn't be treated like some sort of wayward child for something that was so wholly out of my control. "Now," I said, pointing to the interior of the office.

"I'm not sure what there is to say, Izzy," He mumbled as he made his way in.

"Well, if you don't have anything to say, you can just listen to me." I closed the door and locked it before turning back toward Kennan. "Sit, this is going to take a while." I motioned towards the chair with my head.

"Fine, I'm sitting. What do you want to talk about?" Kennan threw himself into the chair looking at me defiantly the whole way down.

"Really, Kennan? What do I want to talk about? I want to talk about us. I want to know what in the Hades is going on between us. Besides the obvious stuff, the unfixable stuff, something has shifted. Do you not want to be with me anymore?" My eyes brimmed with tears I refused to shed.

"Of course I want to be with you. Don't be ridiculous. It's just...," Kennan trailed off.

"What, Kennan? I've been going crazy these past two months. With everything going on, the one thing that was my constant was always you. Until lately, that is. So, please, just tell me. We can't keep going on like this. I can't keep having to worry that I'm doing something wrong."

"It's just, him. He is always there. He just pops in whenever he feels like you need something and you never once turn him away. But that isn't all, Izzy. I'm starting to wonder if you would rather have this life than the one we had back at the farmhouse. I feel like I'm losing you - losing us."

"I would rather have this life? Really, Kennan?" I could barely keep the anger and hurt from my tone. My chest felt heavy. I couldn't understand it, how could he be so completely wrong? I choked back a sob as I continued, trying to get every word out around my uncontrollable tears. "You think that I would rather be here, getting branded by some invisible force? I didn't choose this life, Kennan. I don't know if you remember this past year all that well, but at no point did I say, 'Gee, saving the world sounds like a terrific new hobby.' I don't want this anymore than you do, but this is where we are. I refuse to let more people get hurt just so that I can be selfish. If you ever knew me at all, you would know that."

"Of course I know you, Izzy!" Kennan shouted, raising from his seat. "I just feel like you took all of this on without any thought to what you were giving up."

"Every second of every day, I think about what that life would've been like. So don't accuse me of not missing it, of not knowing what I've lost." Sobs racked my body as I let everything I'd held back for the past months pour from my mouth. "I miss it. I miss waking up to you in the farmhouse, of feeling safe and blocked out from the world. I miss us. But there is absolutely no way I could ever live with myself if I chose that life when it means letting so many other people suffer." I folded my arms around my stomach, trying to keep the gaping chasm from ripping any wider. I missed Kennan. I missed our old life, but I knew that it was gone.

Kennan moved toward me wrapping his arms around me. "I'm sorry. I just didn't think I would ever have to give you up. I never imagined you would be the girl from the prophecy, Izzy. I've just felt like you've been plowing forward and leaving me behind with your old life, as if you don't need me anymore."

"Don't need you? Have you lost your damn mind, Kennan O'Malley? I will always need you. Always." I wrapped my arms tightly around him, trying to hold on to the only anchor I had in this chaotic world.

"What about him? It seems like you need him more."

"Seriously?" I pushed away from him, anger replacing the hurt that had just been there. His jaw clenched as he stared back, unmoving.

"Yes, seriously."

"First, you should be nicer to him. I wouldn't even be here if he hadn't saved me."

"You wouldn't have died if he had taken better care of you. I think he did it intentionally, Izzy."

"You think that he let me die so that he could change me? That is the most absurd thing I've ever heard, and I've heard quite a few whakadoo things this past year. He saved me, Kennan. And like it or not, that means that part of me is changing. If I want to understand what is happening to me, I have to understand him better. To understand him better, he has to be around. Would you rather my eyes light up unexpectedly in front of the Council?" My anger began coursing through me in discernable waves, traveling down my arms in rapid succession and ceasing at my fingertips.

"Umm, Izzy, maybe you should take a deep breath." Kennan's voice was on edge as he slowly backed away from me.

I looked down at my arms to find little flickers of electricity tracing down them only to culminate at a spark at my fingertips. That explained the wave feeling. Son of a butternut squash.

"Seriously, lightning when I get angry!" I shouted at the ceiling. "I'm going to kill him myself. How the hell am I supposed to hide this?" The angrier I got, the more sparks seemed to fly.

"Maybe try not to think about it right now, Izzy. Go to your happy place." Kennan said, half teasing.

I tried to take deep, calming breaths to get myself centered again, the way Ian had been trying to teach me. I'd always been an overly emotional person; up until now it hadn't been a problem. Unfortunately, a tricky little side effect of this new "change" that was happening was that any time my emotional state became unbalanced a fun new ability would pop up. Breathing in slowly, I mentally wiped away the anger as if it were written on a dry-erase board. The sparks finally quit coursing down my arms.

"I can't do this without you," I breathed out, almost near tears once more. "You're what I need to survive this, Kennan. Without you, I can't make it." I could feel the anger leave my body, only to be replaced by a gut wrenching sadness.

"You don't have to, Izzy. I know I've been acting crazy lately, but I feel like I've been playing catch up since we got here. I just need some time to adjust. Just don't expect me to ever like Aberto. He is up to something where you are concerned and I don't trust him."

"Do you trust me?"

"Of course I do." Kennan leveled me with his eyes.

"Then listen to me when I say that not in a million years could anything ever tear me from you. You are my home, Kennan. You are my shelter from this raging storm. Nothing, and I mean nothing, will ever change the way I feel for you. Even should I live to be as old as Aberto, which now seems possible, I will always love you more than I could ever love anyone. You are my other half, the part of my soul that has always been missing." As the last words left my mouth an image of Aberto danced through my mind. I brushed it to the side, refusing to acknowledge that I literally had his soul inside of mine at the moment. This was a figurative ideal, not literal. Yep, that was my story and I was sticking to it.

"I'll try to be more patient, but I can't guarantee that I will ever be friends with him. I think I might learn to tolerate him. I know that you're where you need to be, I just miss the life I thought we'd have. I am still playing catch-up." Kennan pulled me back against his body, almost smothering me.

"I'm all yours, big guy. No matter what is going on in this insane world that will always be true." My response was garbled by the mouthful of t-shirt I was trying to talk around.

"I wish that we could make-up. Those damned runes are going to be the death of me." Kennan leaned in to gently kiss me, reminding me of everything I was missing thanks to these God forsaken doodles.

I pulled back with a raised brow. "I think you can find some creative ways to avoid them, if you really think about it."

The wind was knocked from my lungs as Kennan pinned me to the couch. He hungrily kissed down my neck, careful to avoid touching any part of me that may have a rune. As he moved over me, a single thought crossed my mind. No matter what he'd said, I knew things wouldn't be getting better any time soon. The more I changed, the more things would continue to shift between us. If he couldn't accept what was happening, I wasn't sure anything would ever get better. I shook the thoughts from my mind and turned my focus back to Kennan's wicked lips. There was no harm in focusing on the present.

Just as Kennan began unzipping my dress, a knock sounded at the door.

"Damn," Kennan breathed. "It never ends." He buried his face in my stomach for a second before getting up and moving across the room.

"What is it?" I choked out, trying not to sound as out of breath as I felt.

"Milady, the Council members are getting ready to depart, and they wish to bid you a proper farewell." Conall's voice sounded strained, as if there were a thousand other things he wished he could be saying about the Council.

"I'm on my way." I stood and smoothed out my rumpled dress trying to rearrange the disarray. I looked up to find Kennan staring at me. "Are we okay?"

"We will be," Kennan promised. "Now, go be the terrifying Council leader I know that you are."

"Pshaw. I wish. Is there some sort of proper way to send off Council members, other than flipping them the bird? Because, that is really all I want to do to them."

"No, just go stand out front as their cars leave. That's what Isadora always did. Oh, and look bored. That always seems to annoy them." Kennan moved toward the door and opened it, waiting for me to pass.

As I entered the hall, I was immediately flanked by Conall and Kennan. We moved through the halls quietly as people paused to bow their heads in my direction. I nodded back to each of them, knowing that I would never truly get used to this sort of attention. I felt like a fraud. As we reached the front of the house, Kennan and Conall fell behind me, allowing me to exit in front of them.

"We bid you farewell," Brutus shouted. I needed to find out screamy-pants' name.

"May God bless your journey. I expect to hear from you soon regarding the darkness. Until then, be well." The words poured from my mouth without thought. It was as though I was channeling Isadora.

"And you, milady," Damali said through clenched teeth.

With that, the four Council members piled into two black sedans and were off. I wasn't sure if I would hear from them or not, but their absence was a relief. The breath returned to my lungs, and the weight lifted from my shoulders. Shaking off the oppression their presence brought with them, I reveled in the fact that I would no longer have to hide what was happening to me. Other than the contacts, I was free.

Well, maybe the sparky thing would have to be hidden. I should really talk to Aberto about that one.

"What is on the agenda for the rest of the day, Milady?" Conall asked, never looking away from the departing cars.

"A nap. Some food. Maybe a little research?" I swayed on my feet slightly, only to be caught by Kennan.

The runes were still taking a heavy toll on me, even with the extra protection that Aberto had applied. I felt tired all of the time, yet I was terrified to go into the dreaming for fear of being marked more. I wasn't sure how much more I could take before I ended up like Cait, Conall's would've-been Seer. The memory of her approaching that monstrous beast skirted through my mind, before disappearing.

"I need to lie down." My voice came out a mere whimper. I had to maintain a strong façade for the Council members, but now that they were gone, I felt the toll the strain had taken.

"Let's get you to bed." Kennan reached around my side to support the majority of my weight as we moved inside the house and up toward our room.

Chapter Five

My feet were lead bricks dragging beneath me as I sluggishly made my way to our room. Exhaustion pulled at me, beckoning with the promise of peaceful rest that I knew was a mere tease. I really wanted to get this whole prophecy thing over with. Maybe in death I would find some rest. Perhaps that was a bit too melodramatic, but at this point, death was definitely starting to have an upside.

"Do you need help getting your contacts out?" Kennan shut the door, pulling me from my dour thoughts.

"Yuck! I don't want your fingers in my eyes." The very thought of it caused my stomach to churn. "I think I have enough energy to handle it. But if you could undo my zipper, that would be awesome." I turned my back towards Kennan. As his hand brushed down my spine, trailing the zipper with it, chills rushed through my body. His lips brushed my neck and traced the line my zipper had just made, causing my toes to curl.

"Kennan, I don't think I can right now. I am so...." I collapsed to the floor leaving the words unspoken. Consciousness had once more eluded me, a circumstance that was unfortunately occurring more and more frequently. Perhaps the runes were to blame, or maybe my body couldn't cope with Aberto's soul residing inside of me, either way, it was annoying. Nothing like a narcoleptic leader to save the day.

Awesome, I was once more in the dreaming. How I'd arrived there was beyond me considering that I'd been doing my durndest to avoid the place. Staring out into the fog, I knew. The menace that lurked within the dark shadows was growing. The darkness beckoned, whispering promises of pain, of unimaginable torments. Shivers travelled down my spine.

I looked around, half searching for Ren's spirit. I'd grown so used to her company in the dreaming, no matter how unpleasant, it seemed strange to no longer see her here. Though I wouldn't wish an eternity in the dreaming on anyone, I selfishly missed the companionship.

I moved through the fog with no real purpose. I'd been pulled into the dreaming for a reason, eventually it would show itself. Here's hoping it wasn't for another rune attack. Yep, that's what I'd dubbed them, much to everyone's chagrin. Rune attack sort of sounded like it should be a punk rock band. Maybe I could get some Guardians together and form one. I moved along, with my ridiculous train of thought for company, for a small eternity. What came before my eyes pulled me to a stop.

I was looking out at myself, a mere image of my childhood form. It was almost transparent, but I was there. I was huddled in a ball crying out for the nightmare to end. I could remember this, I didn't know how, because I thought I'd never been in the dreaming until last year. I was a child, I shouldn't have been here. How could I have forgotten this? I moved toward myself, but as I drew near, another figure appeared causing me to draw in a sharp breath.

Aberto moved towards the weeping child and bent before her, me, whatever. I was starting to get really confused. I moved closer to hear what he was saying. I drew as close as I dared, which seemed to draw his attention. He began to turn and look in my direction, as if he knew that I would someday be there, seeing this *exact event. But just as he began to shift, he turned his attention back to the child version of myself. I moved closer carefully; I needed to know what was happening.*

"Izzy, please look at me," Aberto pleaded softly.

"Where am I? I want to go home," my child-self cried out.

"You are safe. I will always protect you, no matter where you are." Aberto smoothed the little girl's silken, red hair from her face.

"Who are you?" the child asked.

"Someone from your future. Someone you will someday meet. For now, I am the Guardian of your dreams. I am here to protect you from these memories until you are ready. You won't remember any of this when you wake up. You will only remember the sweet dreams that follow. Now take a deep breath and think of the most lovely thing you can imagine." Aberto's voice was gentle as he spoke to the child. He continued to smooth her hair away from her face as he whispered words to send her out of the dreaming and into a restful sleep.

As the image of the girl disappeared, Aberto stood and looked straight into my eyes. I knew then, like I had always somehow known, he'd always been there. But why? What was I to him? As I began to ask him, he reached an arm out pushing a wave from his fingertips that thrust me from the dreaming.

Gasping for breath, I struggled to orient myself. The force of being shoved from the dreaming, along with the implications of what I'd just witnessed, overwhelmed me. My mind began to shift, making space for the memories long forgotten. What else had been taken from me? Were there more memories? Tears streamed down my cheeks as I tried to draw myself back to the present. I was bone achingly tired, yet I didn't want to fall asleep again. I wasn't sure what else might be waiting for me.

"You okay, Iz?" Kennan moved towards me, concern radiating from his body.

"Yeah, just a weird dream, I think. I mean, it must've been a dream, because it wouldn't make sense otherwise. I'm just really tired. Can you whammy my brain? I need to sleep for a while." I took in the sight of my Guardian, tall and strong, everything that had brought me comfort through the past year of upheaval. He'd been my rock for so long, I wondered how he could stand it. Just the thought of having to leave him tore me apart inside. I choked back on the tears that threatened to burst forth. For the zillionth time, I wondered if I were truly strong enough to survive what was coming, or if I would be strong enough to do what needed to be done.

"Hey, Red. Look at me." Kennan sank to the bed reaching out for me in the process. My body curled into his, seeking out his heat, searching for the refuge that had been there all along. I couldn't look him in the eyes, he would know everything just with one glance. "Izzy, look at me."

I turned my face toward his as the tears came unbidden. There was no stopping them, there was no hiding my fear. I wasn't strong enough for this. These runes were slowly killing me, and I could feel it with every breath I took. I wanted to end it all, the darkness, the pain, the suffering, it all had to stop.

"Izzy, what is it? Talk to me, please," Kennan pleaded.

"I'm not strong enough. I can't do it. I can't be the person everyone needs me to be. I could barely hold myself together today, and then I got angry and lightning bolts shot from my fingers. I'm so tired, Kennan. I just want to sleep, but I am too afraid to even do that. I don't know if I can fix this mess, this darkness that seems to be looming, but never clear." I choked back a sob as the words poured from my mouth. Every fear I'd been repressing for the past two months came rushing to the surface at once.

"Izzy, you are the strongest person I've ever known. And you aren't alone, this isn't just on you. You have Ian, Molly, Conall, and me. The Division will also be there to back you up." Kennan paused for a moment as if he didn't want to utter the next words. "And you have Aberto. He's already shown that he will do whatever it takes to protect you. This is not your burden to bear alone, Izzy. Give me some of the weight, or it may just crush you. I know things haven't been easy with us the past few weeks. I haven't been there for you the way that you needed me to be. I'm sorry for that. I truly am. I don't think I realized just how much these changes were affecting you until now. You always seem to be so in control of everything, like you don't need anyone else in the entire world."

"You should know better than anyone that it is a façade, Kennan. I've been trying to fake it until I make it since we got here. Not a day passes that I don't feel completely freaked out by everything going on. The darkness coming, the changes that don't seem like they are going to stop any time soon, not to mention the whole leader of the Council bit, I'm a hot mess right now. I just wish there was some sort of clear outline of what I'm supposed to do. The not knowing is the worst."

"You're always a hot mess, Iz," Kennan snickered, pulling me from my pity party.

"That is a true-fact." I curled myself back into his chest. "How are we going to survive this, Kennan?"

"The same way we do everything. Together. You need to spend some time talking to Aberto. We have to find out what is happening with you. For now, you need to sleep."

The thought of Kennan resigning himself to the fact that Aberto had to be involved was huge. I still hadn't told him about Aberto's confession, and then there was the dream that I'd just had. I wasn't ready to look too close at that. As a thousand thoughts passed through my mind, Kennan began to utter the words that would send me off into a dreamless sleep. Only, it wasn't a restful sleep that awaited me, it was something far worse than memories.

A parade of images passed through my mind, calling forth memories long forgotten. It was as though I were sifting through my own past, searching for answers. At every turn he was there. I was in the dreaming, I was a child playing with my friend the Old One. I was a teenager, freshly struck with the grief of losing my parents. I was in the fog, seeking out Aberto, but not knowing what I was seeking.

It seemed like at the end of each memory, there was a ghost of an image, a whisper that erased the time that I'd passed in the dreaming. Yet, the more I came there, the less afraid I was. I'd been wondering since all this had begun, how I could possibly have adjusted to the dreaming aspect of this world so easily. Now I knew, it was because I'd been there so many times before. I just couldn't remember. I felt a wave of anger wash over me at all of the memories that had been stripped from my mind by Aberto. What right did he have to take them from me? My anger melted away as my memories brought me to a part of the dreaming I hoped never to experience again.

I was back at the lab, being tortured by Xavier. Yet, in these memories, as I was being ripped to shreds by the wolves, resigning myself to death, there was Aberto. But this time, he didn't intercede. He stood on the outskirts of the vision, as if to observe what I may do. I watched myself go through each of the torturous scenarios all over again, each time seeking out Aberto only to find him watching, waiting. Why hadn't he helped me?

By the time the endless parade of memories began to fade, I was furious. He'd left me there to suffer when he could've saved me. He said that he cared for me, but how could anyone that cared for me ever stand idly by while my world was torn apart? Then the last memory of him surfaced, a memory of my last nightmare at the farmhouse. He'd told me that it was time, he'd nudged me into action, into this mess I was in now. Why hadn't he protected me?

Chapter Six

The fitful sleep finally released its hold on me as the sun began to retreat. Darkness was falling and I was left with a thousand questions, and only one person that could answer them. Well, not even a person. Whatever he was, he'd made my "people that I'd like to throat punch" list. In fact, he had moved right up into first place on the list. Sitting up, I stretched my arms high overhead attempting to shake off some of the dreams, memories, whatever they were. I looked across the room to find Kennan sleeping in a chair rested against the door.

"Hey, handsome." My voice came out like sandpaper. I'd startled Kennan from him dreams causing him to almost fall out of his chair. His arms flailed like some deranged cartoon character as he tried to steady himself.

"Um, hey yourself. What time is it?" Kennan rubbed his hand down his face, a sure sign he was worn.

"I'm not sure, but there is someone I need to talk to, and I need you to be cool about me doing it alone."

"Again? Already?" Kennan stood, trying to stretch out his stiff muscles and effectively rerouting my focus. "Izzy?" Kennan's raised brow brought me back to the present.

"Unfortunately. I'm going to head down to the office. If you want to go grab some food, I can get Conall to come stand outside of the office. I know it isn't exactly pleasant for you to have to stand out there while he is in there with me."

"I'm fine, although, I am a bit hungry. Maybe you're right, it might make things easier if I'm not there every time he shows up."

"Are you sure?"

"I trust you, Izzy. Nothing will ever change that." Kennan pulled me close to him, kissing the top of my head.

"Alright, well, let's get to it then. I want to get this over with. I just hope his Oldness doesn't try and play keep-away with the answers again. I'm awfully close to throat punching him right now, so he'd better watch himself."

"You're terribly scary, you know that right?"

"Oh, don't you start with me, mister. I have lightning bolt fingers now. I could totally zap you when make me mad."

"I am truly terrified." Kennan did his best to look afraid, although, I wasn't buying it for a second.

"You better watch yourself. I'll zap you when you least expect it." I raised my brows up and down like some sort of deranged scientist, all while drumming my fingers together. I thought I looked truly frightening. Or insane, but who's counting?

"Okay, fine, you are a fearfully and wonderfully made Seer of limitless talents. Happy now?" Kennan smirked.

"For now," I preened as I walked down the hall toward my office, where Conall just happened to be waiting. Convenient, that.

"Did someone tell you to be here?" I was curious how he'd gotten here so quickly.

"Aberto said that you might be in need of my assistance this evening. He is waiting on you in your office," Conall said with a deep bow.

"Oh that son of a biscuit eating, Old, secret-keeping asshat. I'm seriously going to zap him. He deserves it. The eavesdropping bastard." I started to storm into the office as Kennan pulled me to a stop.

"Breathe, Izzy. You know that half of what he does, he doesn't realize is completely messed up." Kennan becoming the voice of reason was seriously throwing my world off of its axis.

"Um, when did you get on team Aberto? Aren't you supposed to be as pissed off that he was thought-intruding again? Aren't you supposed to be righteously angry about the whole Aberto intruding in our lives bit?"

"I know that we need his help if we are going to make it through this. It doesn't mean I like it, it doesn't mean I like him, it just means that I don't want this to be something that causes more of a rift between us. I need us to be okay, and I know that he has to be a part of our lives now. So, take a deep breath, and go in there with a calm and level head."

Calm and level head, my arse. I wanted to give Aberto the what for, but instead I did as Kennan asked and inhaled slowly, trying to erase the anger. In with the good air, out with the anger, or some nonsense.

"Fine, I'm calm now," I mumbled through gritted teeth.

"Yeah, that's completely believable." Conall's disbelief did nothing to help contain my fury. I eyed him evilly as I slowly opened the door.

"You, I will see in a bit." I eyed Kennan steadily as I slipped through the door.

"Get me when you're done," Kennan answered before turning to talk to Conall.

I entered the office, shutting the door just to lean against it. I glanced across the office to where Aberto stood gazing into the fire. Emotions bombarded me as the memories all scrambled to the surface once more. Joy and anger warred with one another as I looked that the man standing before me.

"Why?" I whispered as tears brimmed in my eyes. The last of the memories surfaced, bringing with them the sting of betrayal. In the lab, he'd done nothing to help me. It was unforgiveable.

Aberto moved towards me more quickly than any human could. He stopped just short of me and raised a hand to brush my cheek, something he'd been doing since I was a child. I pulled away from him, using that same speed to put myself across the room. Well, that was new. Awesome. Just call me Speedy Gonzales.

"Don't." I choked back more tears as they threatened to pull me under. I needed to keep myself together. I needed to know. "You owe me answers, and not just some bullshit this time, Aberto. What in the hell is going on? Why am I remembering you from when I was a child? How in the heck did I get into the dreaming as a kid in the first place? And isn't all of this stuff you think that I should've known? Would you have ever told me if I hadn't started to remember?" I paused looking at the man in front of me. His beauty, even masked by years of loss and sadness, made the betrayal feel all the more fresh. "Why didn't you help me? You were there."

"Because you wouldn't let me!" Aberto yelled, as he rushed forward, crowding me, backing me against the wall. He lifted his hand to my face and everything came rushing back. Every last nightmarish scene played out in my mind as the truth came, sweeping me back into the dreaming to witness them all over again.

The house was burning around me. The flames licked up my legs slowly melting my skin away and as I looked over I saw him standing there, shouting.

"Izzy, let me in," Aberto pleaded from just outside the nightmare.

"I don't know you. You aren't real," I shouted back. "Leave me alone. You're just another form of torture. A promise of help that will never come."

"No, Izzy. You can stop this. You are in control, even here. Be strong."

"GO AWAY!" I shouted, as the flames fully engulfed me. As the vision faded I saw Aberto fall to his knees, pleading with me to let him in.

When I finally came back to the present, I was on my knees struggling to catch my breath. The smell of my charred skin still dusted my nostrils, causing the contents of my stomach to roil. Aberto lowered himself to squat in front of me. He reached up to brush my tangled hair from my face.

"I don't understand." I hoped that for once, Aberto might be able to tell me some answers.

"Izzy," his voice came out part promise, part plea, "you are more powerful than you could possibly know. Even before you began changing, you had the ability to block people out. Just as you blocked your Guardian from the dreaming, you were able to shield yourself from me. I would have gone through hell to drag you out of that torture. There is nothing on heaven or earth that would keep me from protecting you, except you, yourself. Only you have the power to stop me, Izzy. So please, don't believe that I would ever let you suffer if I could end it. I would have taken that burden from you and protected you, my directive be damned. I was under the impression that you understood, where you are concerned, nothing is off-limits."

I stared up into his face, the impossibly tall figure that he was, and I realized that he was right. He would move the heavens for me, and he had. He had changed my fate and turned me into something, something that has never been before or will be again. Tears streamed down my cheeks as the charred smell finally dissipated.

"But what about before, why did you make me forget? How was I there, Aberto? I don't understand any of this. Why would you want me to forget, why not tell me the truth when I first saw you at the ceremony?" I paused, trying to gain my bearings before asking the question that had been on my mind the most. "Would you've ever told me had I not remembered?"

Aberto sighed, dropping his hand to his side and raising to his feet. He turned away from me and paused. "Because you are the prophesied one, you can do impossible things. You've had a presence in the dreaming your entire life, Izzy. But, that knowledge, those experiences, they are not meant for one so young. You would have gone mad had I not interceded on your behalf. Would I have told you? No. I wouldn't have told you, because there was no reason for you to know. What good, what knowledge, and what progress would be gained by you knowing? Nothing. Nothing could be gained from those memories, they were mere chances that we met in the dreaming."

"I would've known to trust you from the start. That's not 'nothing', Aberto." I rose to my feet and moved the two steps that divided us, what seemed a gaping chasm. "That matters. You've been there my whole life, protecting me, even when I didn't know it. So, don't brush that off. Those memories, they were mine. I feel like there is this whole part of my life that has been stolen from me, and now it has all come rushing back in. The flood gates are opened. You had to know that at some point these memories may return, what of the madness that they could bring now? Did you have a plan to protect me from that? Or did you just expect to make me forget again?" The more I talked, the more I became agitated all over again. I had started by trying to reassure him and moved right back into being royally pissed.

Aberto turned to look down at me, his face as still as a statue. "I would do whatever it took to protect you, even if that meant betraying your trust, even if that meant taking memories from you. You can hate me, Izzy. You can be angry with me for taking things from you. I will do it again, and I won't, for one moment, regret it, if it means that you will be safe from the world and yourself. Don't believe that I am like your Guardian, willing to let you put yourself at risk just to make you happy. I will allow you to fulfill your calling, I will do whatever it takes to ensure you can bring the darkness to a halt, but do not get confused, I will not ever allow you to be hurt."

"You owe me answers, Aberto."

"I owe you nothing, Izzy!" Aberto's tone grew cold, rooting me in place. "I have given you everything of myself, yet you still question me. What answers do you want? What is it you think that I am keeping from you? I have told you my darkest secrets, I have told you who I truly am. I can't fathom what it is you think I am not telling you. Do you believe me to have some ulterior motive? I can ensure you, my only motivation on this plane or any other is you."

"Why? Why do you want to protect me? Why have you always been there? What's in it for you? That's what I don't understand. How can you say you have no ulterior motives when you have been there my whole life, protecting me? Surely there is something you want, something you hope to gain from all of this. Otherwise, why even do it? The prophecy says I will fall Aberto, and fall I will if it means protecting the people I care about."

"My motivation has always been you. Someday, you will understand why. But this is not that day. This is not the time."

"Damn you and your 'this is not the time' bullshit. You pulled that on me when we first met, and look where it is gotten me." I lifted my rune covered arms to him as sparks began igniting down my arms once more. "I'm changing into something I don't understand, yet you still won't tell me everything. I can't hide this forever, and when the Council finds out, God only knows what they will do. You do owe me answers, because you did this to me. You changed me, and while I am eternally grateful to still be alive, I don't know what the hell I am now. Because, I'm not human any longer. Not the way I was before."

"I don't know what you want from me." Aberto's voice edged on anger as he closed the gap between us. "I have given you everything of myself. I am cursed to this existence for all of eternity because I interceded. I can never move beyond this existence now for what I did. Quit acting like a spoiled child and act like the Seer you are meant to be. Stop whining about the lot you have been given and embrace it; it may just save your life again. I am through answering your questions. When you are done wallowing in your pit of self-pity, I shall return. Until then, do not call on me."

Just like that he was gone. Poof. The bastard. My anger died a swift death as his words rang in my head. He was cursed to an eternity of what he had been living because of me. I still wanted answers, but I knew deep down that he was right. I had been spending so much time focusing on what was happening with me that I'd once more lost sight of the bigger picture. In the grand scheme of things, lightning fingers weren't that big of a deal. I plopped down into the closest chair, allowing his words to wash over me. I still had no idea how I'd ended up in the dreaming, or why Aberto was there for me. It had not escaped my notice that he was still avoiding the biggest question of all, why he wanted to protect me so badly. But he was right, as he always had been, I needed to pull my head out of my butt and start doing my job.

Chapter Seven

Anger fled my body only to be replaced by the inescapable bone aching exhaustion. I curled into the chair, hoping to find some sort of reprieve from my current lot. I let the dreaming sweep me away, and for the first time I didn't care what I would find there. I went willfully into its foggy embrace, not fearing the runes that may come.

"Fuckskittles, there you are!" A voice rang out from the fog. *"Do you know how long we have been trying to find you, but do you make it easy? Of course not."*

I turned to find a cloaked figure standing in front of me. She was around my height, but the strength she radiated made her presence imposing to say the least. There was something about her that unnerved me, not just her demeanor. The chaotic power pulsing from her set me on edge.

"Ummm, sorry?" I wasn't sure why she'd been looking for me. For all I knew, she was with the bastards that were summoning the darkness.

"Not cool, I'm so not with those asshats. Bureaucratic bullshit, if you ask me. Nope, I'm part of what your people call the Abominations. Which really, when you think about it, is just plain mean."

"Abominations?" Okay, that handbook I'd been meaning to write since all of this happened, it was going to have to be extra-long. I was constantly learning new things. This Abomination business didn't sound too promising. In fact, I wasn't sure talking to someone that was considered an abomination of any sort was a good idea.

"Yeah, the group of Seers and Guardians that choose to use their abilities for what they were meant for, instead of seeking the approval of the Council before moving forward with their actions. You know, Seers that operate outside of the regulations? I guess you could call us rogues for the side of good."

"I didn't even know there was another group of Seers. I thought that this was pretty much it."

"Where have you been? Seriously? We don't have time for this. You need to come to us, we have information for you. We've been trying to find you for weeks, but something has been blocking us. So talk to your Guardian, or whoever you trust, and come find us."

"Who are you?"

"I'm Sena, the Grand-Seer's messenger. Find us, Izzy. You're gonna need our help. Until then, protect yourself, because not everyone is who they seem to be."

"Yeah, I pretty much figured that one out already. Where can I find you?"

"Your Guardian will know, and if not, ask your Old One. He can certainly bring you to us. Oh, and tell old Abe I said hey."

"Ummmm," I said as I stared at the empty spot where Sena had just stood. Had she seriously just called Aberto "Abe"? I couldn't see him liking that at all. And what in the heck did fuckskittles even mean? Whoever Sena was, she sure had a foul mouth, but I liked her.

I walked around the fog for a while, aimlessly. I wasn't sure what I was looking for, perhaps it was Aberto. Perhaps, I just wanted to find the bastards that kept marking me up with runes. I let my mind wander and memories wash over me. Things would never be easy for me again, of that I was sure. Aberto had been right, it was time for me to stop wallowing and accept that some things just were. Waiting for him to explain *anything was rather fruitless at any rate. He wasn't exactly the most open person. I thought about Sena as I walked. I wondered if she was just another trap, or if her people really had information for me. Ultimately, there was only one way to find out, and I wouldn't find it in the dreaming. At least this was something proactive for me to do.*

I came back to the present feeling empowered by the thought of having something to do. I had been spending countless hours with Eleanor going over musty old documents with not so much as an idea of how to put a stop to the darkness to show for it. I was tired of not being able to fix whatever was coming, and more importantly of not knowing what exactly was coming. I knew one person that could help me, but drudging up her ghost seemed cruel. Cait had suffered enough, and if I could find a way to put an end to all of this without her help, I would. I looked around the room and found Kennan standing next to the door staring at me.

"How long was I out?" My voice was raspy from sleep.

"Just an hour. Aberto popped out in the hall before he left. What did you do to make him so angry?" Kennan moved towards me slowly, questions lingering in his eyes.

"Nothing, it was totally not my fault. He has his stupid secretive self to blame for that." I sat up straight then bent over stretching out the stiffness that had settled in my muscles.

"You were talking in your sleep. Were you in the dreaming, or was it just a normal sleep?"

"The dreaming. I honestly don't remember what a normal sleep is like. But, I may have some good news. Probably." I paused looking up at him. Only hours ago things seemed to be getting better between us, but I could tell that the rift was still there. It was smaller, but it was not gone. My heart dropped for a moment before I pulled my attention back to the bigger picture. I didn't have the luxury of worrying about myself anymore. It was time to get proactive. "Do you know someone called the Grand-Seer? Or maybe where I can find the Abominations?"

"Why would you want to see them? They have forsaken our cause to fulfill their own desires." Kennan spat. Apparently, he held the same view of these people that everyone else in the Council did. As far as I was concerned, they were just Seers doing what they were called to do. But what did I know?

"They have some information for me. They told me to come and find them, and I intend to."

"You can't trust anything they say, you know that right?" Kennan moved to kneel in front of me. "Anything they tell you will probably be misleading and just take us on a wild goose chase. They can't be trusted."

"Have you ever met them?"

"No, but that isn't the point. I know of their kind. I've heard the stories."

"So, you're telling me that in all of your years you have never interacted with them at all, yet you can adamantly declare that they are up to no good? I find that hard to believe from someone like you. What happened to the Kennan that thought for himself and gave people the benefit of the doubt?"

"He realized that he was naïve and foolish. You almost got killed by my brother thanks to my forgiving nature. Pardon me if I am leaning towards the side of caution these days."

"I have to find them, Kennan. If they can help me, then I need to go. I already know that there are people here I can't trust. Even if I have no clue who they are.

Isadora really could've given me a heads up on that one." I paused looking down into Kennan's worried eyes. "We have to do whatever we can to make it stop. Even if that means going to find people that y'all seem to think are going against some sort of divine manifest. After talking to Aberto, I am starting to think that none of y'all really know what you are here for. So, I'm not going to pass any sort of judgment until I meet them for myself. Will you help me, or not?"

"Of course I'll help you. Unfortunately, the Grand-Seer keeps them on the move. She is notoriously untrusting of anyone outside of their Order. The last time I heard, they were in South Dakota near the Badlands. They tend to hide themselves in places that are hard to find. Ian may know more. He was sort of raised inside the Order."

"I thought you and Ian had known each other for like, ever. What do you mean, he was raised inside the Order?"

"I mean, his mom was a member. They don't demand that you stay there, they give you a choice of where you feel you most belong. If nothing else will dissuade you from finding them, just remember how weird he turned out." Kennan rubbed a hand down his face in exasperation.

"I'm going to go find Ian. You coming?" I got up and headed towards the door, not even waiting for a response. I was getting better at the whole Isadora question thing.

"I suppose I don't have any other choice." Kennan followed closely behind until we reached Ian and Molly's room. Well, Molly's room that Ian had been camping out in since her mom had been brought in. Ian didn't trust Molly to go unsupervised while her mom was in the same house. I was convinced that

Molly would have shanked her mom by now if it weren't for him. "Don't say I didn't warn you, Izzy. Most of the stories I've heard came from Ian."

"Yeah, yeah. Stop stalling. I finally have something that I can do, and here you are trying to keep me from it."

"Woah there, scrappy. I'm not trying to keep you from doing what you need to. I'm just trying to be the voice of reason. Remember, I'm supposed to be keeping you sane?"

I glared at him a moment before turning my attention back to the door. Just as I raised my hand to knock, it opened with Molly staring at me.

"Are you going to stand out here yapping all night, or come in?" Molly huffed.

"We're coming, settle down." I walked past her into the room, bumping her arm so that she was thrown off balance. I snickered as Ian swept in to steady her.

"I wouldn't have fallen." Molly sounded exasperated. I was sure the close quarters with Ian weren't doing anything to calm her already fragile nerves.

"No harm in being careful," Ian replied steadily. Sadly, Ian had begun dressing in more subdued clothes that matched. He'd forsaken his Hawaiian shirts in favor of button ups, and his kilts in favor or jeans. These were sad times, indeed.

"What can we do for you? I'm sure this isn't a social visit, with everything else that is going on." Molly walked across the room and lowered herself to the bed, patting the space next to her for me to come and sit. I felt a pang of guilt as I moved towards her. With everything that had happened over the course of the last year, she'd always been there for me. Yet, when she needed me the most, I had to keep the rest

51

of the world grounded and didn't have time to be there. It royally sucked. She never once made me feel guilty, she didn't have to. I did a good enough job of that on my own.

"Actually, it is Ian that may be able to help." I lowered myself to the bed, eyeing Ian steadily.

"Oh, really? Do tell," Ian crooned.

"I need to find the Order. They have some information that I need to know. A Seer named Sena just found me in the dreaming and told me to come find them. So, find them I will." Ian's face was a barely contained mask. Just below the surface, a million emotions passed, all conflicting. "Kennan told me that you might be able to help find them."

"Kennan should have kept his mouth shut," Ian said, before turning toward the door.

"Ian, wait. I don't know what happened to you, or why you chose to leave there. I have no idea what reservations you have, but if this can help me put a stop to what's coming, I have to try."

"I'm not going back there, Izzy. I can't go back. Once you make the decision to leave, you are forgotten from the collective. That is their way. So, even if I wanted to help you, I can't. I made my choice when I was young, and dumb, and there is no taking it back. Not even when I wanted to say goodbye to my mother as she died, not when I questioned my decision to leave, not when my whole world fell apart, and not now. I'm sorry, but I can't help you." Ian never once turned back to face me as he said it, instead he just quietly left the room with us all gaping at his back.

"Um, anyone care to explain?" Molly asked, getting up to move toward the door.

"Apparently, Ian was raised by the Order. And I need to find them."

"Well that explains why he is so weird. I'm going to go find him. You know who will have the answers, Izzy." Molly gave me a look before turning to find her Guardian.

"She's right, you know?" Kennan muttered.

"Shut it, you," I groused before getting up to leave Molly's room. It felt weird to be there without her or Ian. "I guess I better get this over with. I'm going to go outside to call for him."

"There's two feet of snow out there, woman. Why can't you do it inside?"

"Because, I'm still irritated with him. I hope he shows up unprepared and freezes his eternal buttocks off. It would serve him right."

"Whatever you say," Kennan snickered as he moved towards our room to grab my heavy coat.

Chapter Eight

I walked out into the frigid Illinois winter, the snow crunching beneath my shoes. There was something disarmingly peaceful about the winter. Everything was at rest, waiting until the cold passed to wake up in the spring. I wished I could do the same, just cover myself in a blanket and wait out the storm. I sighed, causing a puff of smoke to form in the air. I'd wasted enough time. Exhaustion was once more creeping in, and I'd yet to find where the Order was.

"Aberto, I need your help," I whispered to the air. I stood in the garden hedges alone, in the same spot he'd confessed his feelings only months before. Kennan had told me if I wanted to be petulant, I had to do it on my own. He was waiting inside the warm office, where he could still see me.

"Are you done?" the wind whispered. I'd found out recently that Aberto could be on both planes simultaneously. He thought it was hilarious the first time he talked without actually being on this plane. He'd scared the living daylights out of me. I almost felt like Alice when the Cheshire cat would pop in and talk without being there.

"This isn't about that. It isn't even about me so much as information that I was given. I was told to ask Abe for directions," I snickered remembering Sena's nickname for Aberto.

"I abhor that name. Why she cannot call me by my given name, I will never understand." Aberto appeared before me, wearing a dark wool pea coat, buttoned up so that the collar slightly flipped up, framing is ridiculously gorgeous face. I guess my plan for freezing really didn't work out.

"I need to find the Order. Can you help me? Kennan says they move a lot, but Sena told me they have information that may help me."

"Yes, I know where they are. We can go through the dreaming to get there, or we can travel with a large party. It is up to you. I prefer the first, so that we may get there more swiftly. I leave the decision to you, Milady." Aberto turned and walked down the hedges. Something had shifted between us. Since I'd spiked his anger the last time I'd seen him, he'd become cold with me. On the one hand, it might be nice to have the intensity turned down a bit. On the other hand, I was getting sick of moody men in my life. Between Kennan and Aberto, I felt like I was surrounded by a bunch of hormonally imbalanced women. I was getting ready to hand them both their own carton of ice cream and a box of tampons and tell them to both suck it up. Even I didn't get that moody. "Izzy?"

"Right, sorry. Let me go discuss it with Kennan. If you would like to follow me, you are more than welcome to. We might be able to leave faster if you don't poof off again." My feet followed the winding path back up to the house and the French doors of my office. I stepped inside to find an incredibly handsome Guardian waiting by the fire. Oh wait, it was just Kennan.

"Can he help?" Kennan asked, not turning from the flames.

"Yes, he can," Aberto's voice rumbled from far too close behind me.

"So, we have two options. We can all go, posse style. Or, I can go with Aberto on a soul walk into the dreaming to find them. I wanted to see what you thought before I made my decision. I'm leaning more towards the soul walk."

"Wait, you are actually asking for my input before jumping into something? Is this April first? Am I on some reality show right now?" Kennan's face titled up in a half smile which made me want to smack him all the more.

"You're a regular comedian. Now tell me...what do you think?"

"Personally, I would rather be with you when you go. Practically, I think it would be best for you to go through the dreaming. Even if I hate the idea of soul walking, it is the best option." Kennan turned to look Aberto in the eyes fully. "Just try not to get her killed again, okay?"

"I will do whatever it takes to make sure she fulfills what is asked of her," Aberto responded coldly.

Kennan raised a brow in my direction to which I shrugged my shoulder. I didn't have time for his man-drama.

"Welp, let's get a move on. Shall we?" I settled down into the couch, ready to pull my two halves apart. "See you soon."

"Promise me you will be careful this time. No risks, Izzy. I mean it. You take care of yourself."

"Promise, promise!" I muttered.

"You better," were the last words I heard as I pulled myself in two, leaving my corporeal form to lie on the couch as I walked into the dreaming with Aberto.

"Where exactly are we going?" I asked Aberto as he reached for my hand.

"Right now, they are shacked up somewhere in the Okefenokee Swamp. Hold tightly, this journey will not be a pleasant one for you."

"Shacked up? Really Aberto? Did you start reading the urban dictionary online or something?"

Aberto stared at me coldly. Right, I'd forgotten, he was still pissy with me. No jokes today, nope, not gonna happen.

I entwined my fingers with his, my hand swallowed inside his massive one, almost disappearing. The dreaming spun past us in a flurry of images, some real, some imagined. Places, times, they all seemed to merge and divide so quickly I was left reeling by the time we came to a halt. I fell to my knees, trying to breathe deeply to chase away the nausea.

"We're here. We must leave the dreaming to speak with them. For that, you will need to make yourself corporeal. Will this be a problem?"

"Can I have like two seconds here? I feel like my stomach is trying to climb its way out of my body at the moment."

"I thought we agreed that you would not call on me until you were done feeling sorry for yourself." Aberto's cold voice rang in my ears making me want to throat punch him. He was really starting to grate on my nerves.

"Listen here, Old Man. I'm not used to doing some weird time tunnel vortex through the dreaming. I'm sorry if I'm not as up to speed as you would like me to be, but trying to have a second to catch my bearings is not feeling sorry for myself. It's called self-preservation, you asshat." I stood, glaring at him. The green pallor of my skin probably took away from the overall affect, but I was sticking with it. At least my fingers were getting zappy, that was a bit intimidating.

"I have no time for your ridiculous rantings. Calling me illogical names will do nothing to solve our current predicament, Izzy. Now, can you do what I asked of you, or not?"

"I've never tried it before, so I. DON'T. KNOW!" I shouted. I was so tired of his mood swings. I was worn to the bone, nauseous, and unsure of what I was about to walk into. The least he could've done was be supportive.

"My apologies. We will try it now, and see if you are able to do it. Just imagine yourself becoming whole as you enter the next realm. It will be a projection of the real you. If you are unable to do it, I can pass messages between you and the Order." Aberto threw his hand out in my direction. I reluctantly grabbed it and allowed him to pull me through to the other plane, somewhere in the swamps of Georgia.

I mentally tried to feel myself forming a whole being as we passed into the next plane. As the last of the dreaming faded behind me, I could hear a loud "Pop."

"Well done, Izzy." Aberto released my hand, and I opened my eyes to find a whole room of women gawking at me.

"Umm, hi?" I stammered.

"Well, that was fast," Sena said with a smirk. "How's it cooking, Abe? Learned any new tricks? Thrown any more wrenches into the Big Man's plans?"

"It is always a pleasure, Sena." Aberto ground each word out through gritted teeth.

"Don't mind Old Abe, he is just a grump. I think it is all of the years he's spent in the dreaming not getting laid," Sena stage whispered.

"Umm, okay?" I wondered when I would stop stammering. These women probably thought I was a poor excuse for a savior if they'd ever seen one. They were right.

"I guess you want to talk the Grand-Seer, right?" Sena had started speaking slowly to me, as if I were having trouble catching up.

"Yes, the Grand-Seer, right. That would be awesome. Knowledge is power and all of that."

"Well, follow me then." Sena moved off hollering at everyone to stop gawking as we went.

I finally began to take in my surroundings. We were in what amounted to some sort of old house that had been left to the elements for God only knew how long. The floor boards creaked and moaned beneath my feet as I went, sending out yells of anguish. We made our way towards a dilapidated staircase, which Sena began climbing immediately. She moved fluidly up the stairs with Aberto close behind. I eyed them warily, taking my time to carefully place my feet the entire way up. I wasn't about to let a rickety staircase be my demise. No way, no how.

When I finally reached the top, Sena was busy yapping at an exasperated Aberto. I thought it served him right. In all honesty, it seemed like Sena was doing it to intentionally annoy him. She seemed to like getting a rise out of people.

"Right this way, if you don't mind." Sena led the way down the hall to what must've once been the master bedroom. "She's been waiting for quite a while."

I walked into the room and froze. Sitting before me alive and well was my mother. My knees threatened to buckle as my stomach churned. I blinked rapidly, doing my best to erase the image. Surely this was a mistake. This couldn't be. My mother was gone. She was dead. What sort of hell had he brought me to?

"Oh, dear. You didn't tell her, Aberto?" The painfully familiar voice moved towards me in a flash, steading me as the world tried to flip upside down and shake me off.

"Izzy, I didn't think. I apologize. This is the Grand-Seer. She also happens to be your aunt." Aberto's voice was muffled inside of my ringing ears.

"I'm sorry, my what? My aunt?" I paused trying to get the air to return to my lungs. I was sure my body was going to feel this when I got back. "I don't have an aunt. Especially not one that looks just like my mother. What kind of game is this?" I pulled away from the woman trying to embrace me. I was tired of surprises, tired of tricks, and more importantly tired of everyone keeping secrets.

"This is no game. Your mother chose to leave here when we were young. She saw what had to be done, and what her life must be to bring you into the world. As far as she was concerned, she no longer had any family when she left here. It is our way, Izzy. It is how we have lived for thousands of years, constantly running from the scrutiny of the Council. If we kept in contact with anyone that decided to leave and join them, they could be used to find us. We do this to protect ourselves, and our beliefs."

"But, you look," I struggled to breathe, barely getting the words out, "just like her." Tears flowed down my cheeks. Nothing made sense.

"We were twins, dear one." My supposed aunt lifted her hands to cup my face, before gently placing a kiss on my forehead. "There will be time for answers later. For now, you must know the warning we were given. A warning meant for you alone."

"Just tell me. I really feel like I need to get back to my body soon." The exhaustion pulled at me. My emotions were in turmoil as a thousand questions raged inside my head. But, much like Aberto, this woman seemed all too willing to let me wait them out.

She nodded once before she blankly stared ahead. In a matter of seconds she became nothing more than a mouthpiece. It was the creepiest thing I'd ever seen, and I'd seen some pretty creepy crap over the past year. Her voice came out booming, a voice that in no way could ever belong to her.

"Stop the darkness, or the world shall fall. Seer, you have been changed beyond recognition. You were never meant to be, yet always meant to be. For the price of what you've been given, you must pay. You will fall, but in your fall, you will save them from darkness. Seek out your strengths, use your allies, and wage the war that must be waged." There was an audible snap as my alleged aunt came back to herself.

"That is the worst. I hate when the Big Guy does that." She shook herself as if trying to brush off whatever remained of the message.

"Umm, so was that God just talking to me?"

"One of them. Or maybe it was one of the chief angels. I'm never really sure who is going to use me as a mouthpiece. It is a most unfortunate talent to be blessed with," she said the last part loudly towards the sky, as if the gods cared what they did with her.

I was beginning to resent them. It felt as if we were nothing more than pieces in their grand game of chess. And endless cycle played out between heaven and hell with no real winner. I didn't want to play anymore. I didn't want to be locked in a stalemate with no hope to escape. I began to panic.

Reality slipped through my fingers like so many grains of sand snapping me out of my corporeal form. I needed to get back. I needed to be in my body, away from here. My mind raced in a panic. I looked up at Aberto, breathing out once, before I felt myself pulled into the dreaming. I heard him shout my name as I slipped back, pulled by some invisible string into the fog. I couldn't tell if I'd done it in my panic, or if it was something altogether different.

Chapter Nine

"ABERTO!" My panicked voice rang out, echoing eerily through the fog. "Fantastic, just freaking awesome. How in the hell am I supposed to get back now?" I mumbled, making my way through the fog.

An overwhelming sense of oppressions swept over me as I ran through the fog. Every moment of the past few years played out in my mind as I sought my way back home. Moments of fear and pain, moments of sadness, they all coalesced, forming an impenetrable wall. It was too much; the changes happening within me, the secrets, the terrifying truth of what my future may hold; and as my strength depleted, I began to fall. My resolve fled me in an instant, leaving me to the unpardonable truth. My death beckoned me, pulling me deeper into the darkness. Lost to the world, I fell to my side. The truth settled around me like a cocoon. I would never be enough.

As I let the inevitability sink in, I heard it. A familiar voice called out of the fog. A voice I hadn't heard for two months, yet there he stood. The culmination of nightmares and fears wrapped into the body of a cloaked figure. My future cradled in the palms of his crushing hands. Motionless, I was rooted to my place. The unchangeable darkness, the coming storm, it all pushed down upon me.

He moved towards me, cutting a path through the fog to stand above me like some sort of centurion. The robe covered all but his sneering mouth. The mouth that housed the words that would end me. "Do you see it now? The inevitability? This world will burn for its sins, Izzy. These people, they don't deserve the grace *they are given, or the protection of our kind. Why not just join us? Fighting really is futile."*

The hopelessness pushed against me, prodding me, taunting me. Swallowing deeply, I rose to my knees. I'd never been a quitter, I wouldn't start now. I'd been warned that the darkness would call for me, that it would tempt me. Strength I didn't know I possessed rose up within me. Whatever this person was doing, I could fight it. I could fight him. Taking a deep breath, I stood on shaking legs to face the robed figure.

"I will do everything in my power to protect this world from whatever it is you are trying to bring."

"Look down at your leg, Izzy. Do you really think that you can stop us? Just two more runes and the bridge will be complete. Your fight was lost before it began."

At his words, the burning began on my calf, ripping deep into my soul. I knew that when I awoke, I would have another mark. I wondered if this one would be my undoing. My rubbery legs failed me, and as I began to fall I heard a laugh.

"I will die before I let you do this."

"Yes, you will. But really, your death won't do anything to stop the darkness. It shall end all." He paused, turning back towards me as the fog engulfed him. "Not even Aberto can save you from this." His voice dripped with distain, his words echoing through the fog as he faded away.

"Yeah, fat lot of good he's done me lately," I muttered miserably. I sat there, thinking about the man that had been there. I needed to get back to my body. Eleanor and I had some more searching to do. I thought about my body, laying in the office. Breathing deeply, I closed my eyes. "Please let this work."

The dreaming spun around me quickly as I was thrown out into the office where my body rested.

Conall, Kennan, and Aberto were all there shouting at one another. As I made my way on unsteady legs back to my body, Aberto turned towards me. The fear in his eyes was unmistakable.

"She has returned," he said, moving towards me as I mended my battered soul back into my body.

"Izzy, what happened?" Kennan knelt by me as I struggled to open my eyes.

"Another rune, I have an aunt, Aberto is a giant liar face, secret keeping, butt munch," I muttered almost incoherently.

"Milady, you are speaking in riddles. What happened? Have you been marked again?" Conall assessed me, trying to find where I'd been marked.

I lifted my right leg and pointed lazily at the calf that was now caked in blood. I was so tired of these jerks ruining all of my clothes. I'd only packed three pairs of jeans, and this was the second pair they'd ruined.

"It must be treated," Aberto, the obvious, said.

"Where were you?" I looked at him, struggling to stay conscious. "I called for you."

"I couldn't find you, Izzy. You were blocking again, or they were. I am not certain." His eyes filled with remorse and unuttered apologies. "Rest now, there will be time for answers later."

"There's no time for rest." Tears filled my eyes as I choked back the reality. "It's coming, there are only two runes left before it is here. Whatever they are summoning, it is meant to make people pay for their sins. They don't believe the world is deserving of protection, so they mean to punish it. We can't let that happen. There isn't time to sit here and rest. Something has to be done, a price must be paid. You heard what she said, Aberto. The cost of what you did is that I must fall." My panicked voice rose to a pitch.

"No." Aberto stood abruptly. "NO!" His shout rang through the office, shaking the walls. "It was not her doing. Why must you always ask the impossible?" Aberto's voice echoed, reaching the heavens themselves.

"Enough." Kennan brushed the hair out of my eyes. "This isn't helping anyone. Izzy, you need to rest. I know that you want to get moving, that you think if you take any time for yourself that people will be hurt. I'm here to tell you, if you don't take some time for yourself, you won't be strong enough. One night will not hurt you. Rest now, and in the morning we will search for answers."

"Forgive me," Aberto said as he faded into nothing.

"Izzy, you need to treat this." Conall's voice dragged me from my fuzzy thoughts.

"Bring me the stuff." I looked up at Kennan. The worry in his eyes broke me.

Conall brought the first aid kit, well the Guardian's version of one, over to me. He pulled out everything I would need to treat the wound as I rolled up my pant leg. There on my leg was a rune I hadn't seen before. If only this one had appeared two months ago. Then maybe we would've known that whatever was happening to me had nothing to do with the other Seers dying. Hindsight was for the birds.

I got busy cleaning my leg as Kennan pulled Conall to the side. Their faces were somber as they discussed the transpiring events. They'd seen this before with Cait, and I knew that watching me go down the same road was tearing both of them apart. Seemingly forgetting my new super senses, they carried on a conversation they seemed to believe me unable to hear. Doing my best to act as though I couldn't hear every word, I smoothed on the healing cream.

"She is fading fast. We must act soon." Conall's voice was strained.

"She doesn't know about any of that yet. She doesn't need to know. Not now. It won't do her a bit of good. When the time comes, we will do what we must." Kennan's hand lifted to his face as he turned to look at me. It seemed I wasn't that great at eavesdropping after all. Multi-tasking had never really been my thing.

"Izzy, you need to rest now." Kennan moved across the room to smoothly lift me from the couch.

"Okay." I knew he was right. I needed to sleep in a bad way. The rune could wait until the morning. The explanations could wait for a few hours. I would be absolutely no good to anyone if I didn't take better care of myself. "I'm ready. Can you block me, please?"

"Of course." Kennan's lips moving soundlessly against my hair was the last thing I felt before I slipped into oblivion.

Chapter Ten

Was this the dreaming? No, it couldn't be. After all, Kennan had blocked me. I took a wary step, unsure of where I may be. The surroundings drew me in like a warm blanket, a reassuring weight. The fog drifted around my ankles as I moved through, growing ever closer to the source of comfort, the beacon that drew my soul. The voices grew louder as the fog parted, revealing my mother and aunt. Leaden feet pulled me to a stop as I struggled to gasp for air. It was a memory, a glimpse at something long past.

"Why must it be her? Surely there is some other way. Some way for me to take her place," my mother pleaded.

"Look at her, you know it must be this way. You've been with her since her first breath, surely you knew that her life would not be like that of any other Seer." My aunt pointed out into the fog at a child playing. I looked more closely at the joyous figure until the truth finally settled in my bones. "She's been jumping into the dreaming since she first began to dream. More time will pass, more memories will form. Her sanity is set on a precarious ledge. You must protect her. You must protect yourself. She must come of age."

"Oh, stop being a mouthpiece. This is my daughter we are talking about. How can you ask me to sacrifice my only child?"

"We ask that you sacrifice so much more. You must give her a life separate from your kind. Raise her in ignorance of what she is, yet protect her. When the time comes, you must leave her. This is not a choice. If you do not do this, the world will fall to the darkness. She will either be this world's savior or downfall. Failure

to do as we ask will result in a world filled with chaos and destruction."

"But why?" Sobs racked my mother's body as she struggled with words that refused to sink in. Broken, my mother sobbed, unable to keep the hurt from her face, unable to be strong. I looked at her, wondering how she could've written me letters hoping for a good life, a life separated from this when she knew. She'd always known. Perhaps it was denial, perhaps fear, either way I resented the hope they represented and the life that might've been.

"Why is not for you to understand. It must be so." My aunt shook herself as if trying to get rid of the last bit of whatever had been speaking through her. "I'm so sorry." Her voice barely rose above a whisper.

"Promise me, promise you will protect her. If I must leave her, then you be there. You find her, and you take care of my baby for me."

"I promise. But I don't think that she will be friendless in this world, my dear sister." My aunt nodded towards the little girl. There, playing ring-around-the-rosie, was Aberto. "I do believe that the Old One will guard her well."

"But why? Why does he show such an interest? Can he be trusted?" Score one for mom, at least she wasn't as accepting of him as everyone else seemed to be.

"I will never understand the reasons of the Old Ones. Can he be trusted? I suppose we will have to let time tell. We must go now. People mustn't know that we are still in contact."

"I know. I miss you. Just know that I will haunt your ass if you don't take care of my baby when I'm gone."

"I said I promise, now go get the Old One to wipe her memory. You know what the big chiefs said. She can't know what she is."

"Will I see you again?"

"I don't know. I pray that the gods allow it."

"As do I." My mother hugged her sister tightly. Hesitant to let go, she finally closed her eyes and pulled away to move towards Aberto. "I need you to erase any memory she may have of the dreaming or what she is. She can't know until she comes of age. Can you do this for me?"

"I can. She will resent what has been stolen." Aberto's face looked forelorn.

"It is the will of the gods, God, whoever is using my sister as a loudspeaker."

"Then so be it." He paused for a moment, turning to look at the happy girl skipping around the fog. "Izzy, come here for a moment." My feet carried me closer towards the memory.

"What is it, Aberto? Can we play some more?" My child-self pleaded.

"No, Izzy. Now it is time for a different game. This is a game of memory. I am going to hide memories so that someday, when you need them, you may find them. Does that sound like a fun game?" The child's eyes lit up as she nodded. "Izzy, the dreaming will be no more for you. You shall not remember your friend from sleep, nor shall you remember that your mother can come here as well. The dreaming is but a hazy memory locked away tightly. There is no dreaming, there are no people with special powers, and you are a normal little girl with a grand imagination. Do you understand?"

"Who are you?" the little girl asked. Aberto's eyes clouded over with a look that I had come accustomed to. He had lost something that brought him joy, and it had been replaced with yet another burden to bear.

"It's time to get you tucked in, my sweet." My mother held her hand out for the child. They walked hand in hand, disappearing into the fog, leaving Aberto and I standing there.

"Not everything is always so simple, Izzy. There are times when there is no clear right or wrong, only what must be done. I beg forgiveness for what you feel I have stolen, but I cannot apologize for protecting you. I am honor bound to guard you until my last breath." He was staring straight at me, where I stood.

"How did you know I would be here?"

"I told you, we would play a game of hide and seek. You sought out answers, and you found them. Now, you must wake up. There is much to be done."

"But...."

"Awaken."

I sat up in the bed, trying to catch my breath. How in the heck had I gotten into bed? I looked around the room until my eyes came to rest on the clock and my sleeping Guardian. It was only three in the morning, why in the world had Aberto wanted me to wake up?

"Because we have much to discuss."

"Son of a.... Gah, give a girl some warning, and you aren't supposed to read my mind!" I jumped, waking Kennan up in the process.

"Why are you in our room?" Kennan asked groggily.

"Izzy and I have important matters to attend to. Namely, the darkness. Perhaps you remember, she is the only thing standing between it and the world's undoing."

"There isn't a day that goes by that I don't remember. But perhaps she would be better equipped to save us all if she got a little rest."

"There will be time to rest later," Aberto replied shortly.

"Yeah, when I'm dead," I muttered.

"Not funny," they simultaneously reprimanded.

"Fine, but can I please put on some clothes before we get started? Oh, and maybe drink some coffee?"

"If you must." Aberto moved to lean his mountainous form against the door.

"Umm, turn around." I raised my brows at him, hoping to get the point across.

"You could just conjure some," Aberto mumbled as he turned. I knew that there had to be some sort of a perk to this whole thing. I thought up a pair of pants, but nothing appeared. That trick still needed a bit of work, sad really. I moved towards the dresser and pulled out my last pair of jeans.

Fully clothed, I turned to look at Kennan who was still lingering in bed. "You coming?"

"Am I needed?"

"Pretty sure you are always needed," I answered with a raised brow.

"Not at this juncture. Izzy and I must discuss things she is remembering. The time has come for the rest of our story." Aberto nodded towards Kennan before turning to leave the room.

"You really aren't coming?"

"Izzy, it is easier this way. I know he won't let anything harm you, but when the two of you are together, it is difficult for me not to interfere. He was right, and so were you. I need to let you start standing on your own feet, Iz." The covers fell away from his boxer brief clad body as he got up from the bed to move towards me. "I will always be there when you need me. If you want, I can come now."

"No, I know you're right. But, I don't want you to feel like I'm choosing him over being in bed with you.

Because, trust me, I would much rather be back in that bed wrapped up in you."

"That isn't fair, and you know it," Kennan growled as I tried to climb him. "You know that the risk of transference is too great. Even the times we have tried to be careful, it was almost too close."

Once more, I cursed the blasted runes decorating my body. If any Guardians or Seers touched them, the runes could potentially harness their power to strengthen the bridge. It wasn't a risk either of us was willing to take, but that didn't mean I had to like it.

"This job sucks," I grumbled, disentangling myself from my resilient Guardian. "Moreover, your self-control is stupid."

"Get back to work, oh fearless leader." Kennan swatted my butt before flinging himself back on the bed.

"I don't like you anymore. Just so we're clear," I muttered as I left the room, only to hear a, "You love me and you know it," shouted at my back.

Chapter Eleven

"Alright, spill the goods," I said, limping my sore-legged self into the hall.

"We shall discuss your memories once we have reached the protections of the office." Aberto reached out grabbing my hand inside of his. He pulled me close, helping me to steady myself as we made our way down into the main part of the house where my office was being guarded by a seemingly tireless Conall.

"You know you don't have to stand there all night, right?" I questioned.

"Milady, I wish to ensure that you are kept safe and that your information is uncompromised," Conall's calm voice echoed through the empty hall.

"Right, okay then. Well, we are here now, so go sleep." I moved into the office, wishing desperately that they would put a coffee maker in there.

"Your wish," Conall smiled as he moved down the hall towards the stairs.

"I wish he would stop saying that."

"You are not in high spirits this morning, Izzy. What bothers you?" Aberto moved into the room behind me, pulling the door shut in the process.

"What's the matter?" I groused.

"That is what I am inquiring, what burdens your mind?" Aberto seemed confused as I threw myself onto the closest comfortable surface, which just happened to be the couch.

"No, I'm saying that you should have asked 'what's the matter?' Remember, we are trying to get you hip to the times, old man."

"Ah, I see. What's the matter?" Aberto asked slowly, as though the words tasted strange upon his tongue.

"The dreams, or memories, are they real?"

"They are."

Aberto moved to crouch in front of my prone form on the couch. I rolled to the side so that I could face him.

"Why were you always there? Why was I even there as a child? I thought that wasn't supposed to happen. And my mother and aunt, how do you know them?" I rubbed my eyes, still fighting off the exhaustion that threatened to pull me under.

"You came into this world like a bright shining star, Izzy. There is not one Seer or Guardian in existence that did not feel the moment you came into being. The purity of your life, of your soul, it awakened something in me that I had long forgotten existed. It pulled me from the fog, from the brink of despair, and made me want to be the man I was created to be. You drew me out from the fog, for I knew that I had to rest my eyes upon the being that brought that much light into the world." Aberto lifted his hand to stroke my cheek. This time, I didn't fight him. This time, my soul cried out for the touch. "Then it happened." Aberto paused as if afraid to go on.

"What happened? You are doing the riddle thing again." I raised a brow at him as he stilled his hand on my face staring intently into my eyes.

"I saw you, and everything changed. I knew from that moment that I would do whatever it took to ensure your survival." His voice choked in his throat as he stood to move away.

"Do you regret it? Saving me?" I'd wondered that since he'd told me that he would be stuck like this for all of time.

"Never." Aberto breathed the word, never looking my way. "I would gladly live this unending existence if it meant you were safe. It seems that by interfering I have done you more harm than good. I've put you in this position, owing the gods for something you weren't meant to have. The real question is, how can you ever forgive me? For changing you, for interfering without your consent, I put you more in harms' way, Izzy."

"I'd be dead if it weren't for you." I marveled at Aberto. I'd never once regretted being saved. I might not like the changes happening, but it was way better than being dead. I struggled to pull him back from his dark thoughts. "Don't get me wrong, some days death seems like it would be an easier choice than trying to suppress these new abilities. Then there is the whole ouchie rune thing, that kind of sucks. But, Aberto, I don't blame you for what's happening to me. I just want to understand it. You aren't exactly the most open person I've ever known. Prying answers from you could be an Olympic Sport."

"I don't understand." Aberto looked confused by my reference.

"I'm saying, it is hard to get you to give a clear answer on anything. You have this uncanny ability to steer our conversations in completely opposite directions leaving me unsure of what it was I'd wanted to know. That is, until you're gone again and then I remember what I'd asked you, and what you hadn't answered. So no more misdirection. Tell me about me, about my family. What do you know?"

He turned back towards me, closing the distance between us before he finally began to give me long awaited answers. "As I said before, I wanted to see what brought such a light into the world. I approached your family, stepping out of the fog for the first time in hundreds of years to see you. Many had come to seek my help before, but I'd grown weary of the endless battle. You may imagine the surprise of your father when I first appeared. He'd been there through countless battles with the Division. He didn't trust me, nor did he want me anywhere near his family. He knew that I had the power to intercede on Cait's behalf, yet I had not. Your mother, she was quite a remarkable woman. She convinced your father to allow me to see you. That was the day you came home from the hospital. I walked into your nursery and saw you laying there in the crib, this bright ray of optimistic sunshine and I knew, deep in my soul, that you were my destiny."

"Okay, creepy, but okay, let's move on now." I had a hard time imagining him thinking of me like that when I was a baby.

"I did not see you in that way. You forget that I see throughout time, I could see your life play out in the mere moments it took for you to lift your tiny hand to mine. I saw the tragedy of your parents, of all the suffering that would come to you. I saw everything up until the sacrifices of the Seers. Your life, a series of events that I was powerless to change. Tragedy after tragedy played out, yet after each I saw that the sun still burned brightly. I knew, I would do whatever it took to keep that sun shining. Even if it meant changing destiny and going against the gods."

"Yeah, thanks for that. Did you ever stop to think that if you hadn't interfered, I wouldn't be the one the Prophecy was talking about?" I peered into his face, wondering if anything we did really mattered.

"You have always been the one the prophecy spoke of. Nothing that I have done could change that. I am beginning to believe the gods knew I would interfere long before I did." Aberto perched on the edge of the couch pushing me back in the process.

"Fine, okay, so we are going to get nowhere with that whole line of questioning. Let's move on. What about the dreaming? Why was I there as a child?" I curled on my side to give him more space as he settled in to tell me more.

"The first time you showed up in the dreaming, you were so small. You were terrified. There has never been a Seer born that could travel to the dreaming before they came of age. I felt it, the first day you came. The fog warmed and shifted revealing a bright spot in the haze. I followed it, to find you crying out. That was the first day we played. Entertaining you became the highlight of my existence. You would show up every few days and ask to play a new game. You would teach me things you'd learned from outside of the dreaming. I believe you thought I was your imaginary friend. But things started to change, you started to have visions as a child. Visions that would surely drive you mad. Your mother asked me to intercede. That was the night that you dreamt. The last night we played before I had to make you forget."

"Why didn't my mother stop me from going to the dreaming sooner?"

"Everyone tried. We tried to block you from the dreaming, but it was to no avail. You continued to seek it out, to find your friend. We had no idea that you were trying to find me, until I severed the memories. Then you stopped coming." Aberto's face clouded with loss. I sat up on the couch trying to take it all in. Sitting so close to him that nothing could separate us, the man that had been such a huge part of my life, the man that had been my sanctuary as a child.

"Aberto, why..." I couldn't find the words I wanted to speak. I didn't know how to ask him everything I longed to know. As I struggled to find the words, he reached out to entwine his fingers with my own.

"Izzy, I did what your family asked of me, to protect you. Had I known that I was the reason you kept returning to the dreaming, I would have blocked you much sooner. As for your mother and aunt, how could they know what would become of everyone yet do nothing to stop it? They knew that the darkness that coming was far bigger than any one life. Your life was a precious gift, one they did not want to release, but the gods spoke. Sacrifice is not meant to be an easy thing, and the heavens ask much. They knew, that if you were indeed the one that could stop the darkness, then they must protect you."

I leaned my head against Aberto's shoulder, trying to take in everything he'd just told me. Mister tight-lips had been downright chatty and I wasn't sure how to process everything he'd just said. "So you took the memories of you. My mom and aunt stayed in contact. I have an aunt that is an identical twin to my mom. Oh, and I could walk in the dreaming from pretty much toddlerhood. Is that everything?"

"The important stuff." Which was Aberto for "I'm not telling you everything."

"Fine, so that's been handled. Now we should probably address the whole you getting mad and throwing hissy fits thing. I'm the one that is barely keeping my head above water here. I'm the only one that is allowed to throw crazy emo fits. You're supposed to be the stoic, grounded one of this duo. No more abandoning me, got it?"

"I shall try to endure your endless questioning without losing my head."

"I guess that is good enough. I really need to see Eleanor this morning. Do you think she is awake yet? Oh, and I think Kennan and Conall, heck, why not, the whole gang should be here. I feel a plan coming on, and I think I know just the crazy woman to help us."

"Your plans are not always well thought out, Izzy. Are you sure that you wish to move forward?"

"That's why I am bringing in the committee. I do learn from my mistakes, you know?" I pulled my hand from his, crossing my arms over my chest.

"I shall go and gather everyone. You stay here and rest." Aberto looked completely unfazed by my mini-tantrum.

"You know I still have questions."

"Has there ever, or will there ever, be a time when you don't?"

"Fair enough, now scoot. Oh, and bring me some coffee back when you come, Abe."

Aberto cringed at the name as he got up from the couch.

"Your wish, my command." Aberto raised his brow in my direction as he left the room. Well played, Aberto. Well played.

Chapter Twelve

A small eternity passed as I waited for Aberto to return with the others. The silence crept in, causing my mind to drift to thoughts of Aberto. His motives were still unclear where I was concerned. His reasoning was unfathomable, his desire to protect me unclear. The only thing I was certain of was his sincerity. Deep within my soul, I knew that I could trust him to keep me safe. Every doubt that had wriggled its way through my mind disappeared. Regardless of how confused I was about everything else, at least that was clear.

The door slowly opened, pulling me from my thoughts of Aberto. The people I loved most in the world walked into the office, one after another. They were my posse, my family. It wasn't two years ago that I'd felt so alone with no one but Kennan to call my own. Now, as I looked out at the people filling the room, an overwhelming feeling of comfort swept through me. I was blessed to have people that I could depend on through the worst possible moments in my life. I was blessed beyond compare. No matter what the heavens had in store for me, at least I'd been given some amazing people to help me through it all.

"Why do you look like you're about to cry?" Molly asked lowering herself down next to me on the couch.

"I'm just so thankful for all of you." Tears started to leak from the corners of my eyes.

"Oh, geez. This isn't going to be one of your sap fests, is it?" Ian groused.

"No, it's not." I shook my head trying to pull my attention back to everything else that was going on. "I have a plan."

"May the gods have mercy on us all," Conall muttered.

"Why doesn't anyone have faith in me? A girl screws up once and she is never trusted to come up with a good plan again. Fat lot of good y'all are doing." I crossed my arms, glaring at the people in the room causing them to chuckle. "Fine, you guys figure out this darkness business on your own."

"Izzy, please tell us what you've found," Eleanor said in a slightly scolding tone. She reminded me so much of Isadora. She was so important, and I was beyond thankful that she'd stuck around after the events of the past months. I would've been lost without her guidance.

"Well, first things first." I pulled up my pants leg to show the group my leg. "I got another rune. This one is different from those that were on the Seers, so I'm hoping that it may help us figure out what this group is trying to bring over. The robed dude told me that there are only two more marks left before the bridge is complete, so we really need to figure this out, and soon."

"Cweorth," Aberto whispered.

His voice reminded me of what I'd asked him to bring me back. "Hey, where's my coffee?"

"I am not your errand boy," Aberto grumbled.

"Fine, what does the rune mean?" I would just have to suck it up and go down to the dining hall to get my own coffee.

"It has several meanings. Fire, flame, and transformation are amongst the most well-known." Aberto looked at my leg as if he were studying some ancient text.

"Well, since dude man said that they are bringing forth something to punish the earth for its sins or whatever, it sort of makes sense," I said, pulling my pants leg back over the rune so that Aberto would stop staring at it so intently. The way he kept analyzing me was annoying. "What with the fires of hell and all that. If it is anything like the beastie I saw with Cait, then a demon would make sense. Will this help us figure out what they are trying to bring forth?" I turned to Eleanor and saw that my question had sparked hope in her eyes.

"Follow me." She hurried out of the office and headed to the library, where she'd been spending all of her waking hours combing through books.

"Field trip." Molly's chipper voice reminded me that she was still dealing with a world of hurt. As we made our way out of the office, I pulled her to the back with me.

"How are you doing with everything?" I couldn't keep the concern from my voice.

"It is what it is. Ian has become less of a pain, at least." Molly shrugged it off as if her problems weren't nearly as important as I was making them seem. I knew better.

"I heard that," Ian hollered.

"You were meant to, bonehead," Molly threw back.

"What about everything else? Are you sure you are up to helping with it?"

"There is no way I'm gonna let you do this alone. We are a team! So, stop worrying about me, and focus on you. After all, I'm not the one starting to look like a doodle board." Molly raised a brow looking down at my arms. The tops of my shoulders and back were covered in the beautiful protection marks Aberto had given me. Unfortunately, a bunch of unwanted runes were mixed in with the purposeful ones.

"Some of these were done intentionally," I mumbled. She was right, it was taking me a long time to get used to all of the marks covering my body. I was starting to look like Aberto and his many runic tattoos.

"Fat lot of good they are doing you," Molly replied darkly.

"They are serving their purpose. They have kept her from being marked for two months, have they not?" Aberto sounded defensive.

"So, how did she get marked this time, then? Huh?" Molly was starting to treat Aberto the same way I did, much to Ian's chagrin.

"I believe that I informed all of you that the tattoos were a temporary deterrent. They seem to have found a way around the bindings. Which is why we should be focusing on the future and not what has already passed." Aberto held the door to the library open for Molly and me.

"How are you feeling?" Kennan moved to my side, surprising me. He'd been lingering in the background more and more lately. It sort of reminded me of the way Breanan had always been with Isadora, all lurking in the back, but ready to pounce at a moment's notice.

"Still exhausted, but otherwise not bad. The runes hurt like a mother-trucker, but I can live with it. I just hope that Eleanor can figure out what kind of big bad ugly they are hoping to summon with them. It would be really awesome to not be blindly stumbling about. Maybe with some answers we can finally start being proactive instead of reactive."

"We will figure this out, Izzy. No matter what, you will survive this." Kennan's ferocity was a thing of wonder. He seemed to either be living in serious denial about the prophecy, or he was convinced that we could rewrite my future. I wasn't quite sure which it was.

"Here's hoping," I mumbled. I walked across the room to where Eleanor had set up shop. She was furiously flipping through pages as we approached.

"Found you!" she shouted as she poked the page.

"What, what is it?" I was trying to look over the shoulders of the Guardians surrounding her. I looked like a deranged jack in the box hopping up and down, hoping to get a better look.

"It's not good is what it is," Conall sighed.

"Someone care to share with the group?" I was growing anxious. Based off of the looks Ian, Conall, and Kennan were exchanging, I wasn't going to like what was about to be said.

"They are summoning a demon." Kennan's eyes were filled with terror.

"But I thought Isadora said they weren't exactly demons," I squeaked out.

"They are and they aren't. Demons aren't the sort of creatures that are depicted in the movies. They are harbingers of destruction and chaos, beings created by the depravity of man. To call them demons is to say that they were in existence before man. However, man brought them into fruition. They exist on another plane and those that are unworthy are sent to suffer an eternity under their dominion. It is the equivalent of what you believe to be hell," Eleanor, the ever scholarly, provided.

"So, what is it, what demon are they summoning?" I was far too tired to get a history lesson in what heaven and hell really were. My only concern was what was coming and how to stop it. I could worry about everything else later. If there was a later.

"Sonneillon." Kennan voice was barely audible as he uttered the name.

I was ripped into a vision as soon as the name left Kennan's lips. *Sonneillon, the name, the promise. I looked down at the battle raging below me. The clouds split revealing the demon with a clarity I'd never been afforded until now. I moved down through the parting clouds towards the scene playing out before me.*

The nearer I drew to the demon, the colder I grew. My soul writhed inside of my body, longing to escape the oppressive fear the demon's presence conjured. With heavy feet I moved closer. I had to know. I had to see.

I came as close as I dare to the scene as the demon turned its charred face towards me. I was rooted in pain as the demons features came into full clarity. His skin was a crackling blackened charcoal, split like the ground with no water. A fire raged beneath his skin, turning the cracks into illuminated pools of lava. My eyes scanned up the body of the demon. Every instinct within me shouted for me to not look upon its face directly. I fought the urge to look away and continued to look up and up the giant creature before me.

Four arms chorded in dense muscle stretched out from its sides, culminating in razor sharpened claws. Fighting against every bit of self-preservation, I looked upon the demon's face. His empty fathomless eyes locked with mine, causing me to cry out.

"NOOOOOOOOO!" I fell to my knees as the hate ripped through my soul. Visions flashed before my eyes. Chaos erupted around me, wars raged, and man fought against man. Every image that flipped through my mind brought forth more hate and pain. The emptiness of the eyes, the darkness that walked the earth. It was

too much. It was unbearable. "Make it stop. Make it stop," I pleaded, barely above a whisper.

The sounds of deep sickening laughter ripped through me, forcing me into myself. The pain was unbearable.

"IZZY!" Aberto's shout pulled me from the vision.

I found myself on the floor, curled into the fetal position. Tears trailing down my face as the memories of what the earth would become flashed through my mind.

"What does he want? What is it this demon is meant to do?" I choked out.

"Perhaps you should see this, Izzy." Eleanor moved towards me with the giant tome, handing it to me opened to a picture of the horror I'd just seen.

On the page was a great behemoth of a monster. It stood on two massive clawed feet and rose broadly into the air on backwards hinged knees. Four thickly chorded arms jutted out of its muscular sides, ending in talons. Its head looked to be a combination of a lion and bird with two steer-like horns protruding backwards. The skin was the deepest black I'd ever seen, with a bright fire burning from the inside. The eyes were bottomless pools of fire.

On paper it was nothing more than an image, a snapshot of the horrors that the real thing contained. I quickly closed the book, unable to stomach the picture and the memories it brought forth any longer.

"What will happen if that thing makes it through to this plane?"

"Read this, it will explain everything." Eleanor thrust another manuscript beneath my nose. The pages were yellowed and tearing from the years of use.

I looked down at the pages and held my breath, hoping for the best.

When the darkness falls it shall bring with it the scourge of hatred. It shall turn brother against brother by perverting ideas and conjuring transgressions. Hatred shall spread until the world runs red with the blood of the fallen. The darkness shall fall, and the darkness has a name. That name is Sonneillon, fourth in line for the throne of hell itself.

Weep not for the brothers lost, weep not for the sisters gone, weep for the souls that are left to suffer under the demon's wrath, for none shall survive.

The visions began anew. Neighbor fought neighbor, lover against lover, peace was no more than a memory. Hate saturated the world as every fear was brought forth and manifested tenfold. In that fear there was anger and resentment that could not be pushed down. Emotions ran rampant and all good fled from the world.

I gazed out upon Chicago, a city I'd seen a million times. The roads were covered in bodies of those left for dead. Smoke rose from the skyscrapers that were set ablaze. The city I loved so much was nothing more than a raging war zone. Only, there was no invading country, no true enemy. The truth came rushing in. If I didn't stop this darkness, the world would be no more. Everything I loved, everything I held dear, would be wiped away.

A man ran past me, pure terror etched upon his face. He screamed as a knife flew into his back from somewhere behind me. I turned to see another form moving forward. The man, or he'd once been a man, moved towards his injured prey. A look of delight filled his eyes as he walked more closely towards his prize. He turned his head towards me, sniffing the air as if he could tell I were there.

His eyes locked upon my position and I froze, unable to think. Where his eyes had once been there were now gaping chasms. Black veins moved outward from the sockets moving over his face to form a dark mask. His mouth dripped with black fluid and his words came out a hiss.

"Seer, you aren't strong enough," He slurred before turning toward the man before him. He jumped upon the soon to be corpse and ripped into him over and over again with the knife, giggling maniacally as he worked. The laughter turned my stomach and I sought my way back to the present. This couldn't happen. This had to end.

I was once more curled into the fetal position on the floor. My stomach lurched and I ran towards the closest trashcan, emptying the contents of my stomach. The smell of the burning city still caked my nostrils as the sound of deranged laughter rang in my ears.

"This is the end of the world, isn't it?" I breathed out.

"What did you see?" Kennan moved towards me with a handkerchief.

"I saw what will happen if we can't stop this darkness from coming." I looked up from the trashcan with tear filled eyes. "We have to stop it," I pleaded.

"We will, Izzy, we will." Kennan carefully rubbed my back, one of the few places that was still safe to touch on me.

"Why couldn't it have been just a minor demon? Why does it have to be this one? Are they insane? How am I supposed to fight this? I'm not enough."

"You will not fight alone," Kennan swore. The conversation I'd overheard between him and Conall played back in my head. I wasn't sure what was about to happen, but I knew something bigger than I ever imagined was coming. I also knew I needed all of the help I could get.

Chapter Thirteen

Centering myself, I tried to think. I'd had a plan, I just couldn't seem to remember what it was. With the echoes of hatred ricocheting through my mind I could hardly think. I needed help. That was a start.

"I think that I need to consult the Council members and get their take on this. Does someone have a phone that I can use?" I looked around the room hoping that someone had brought one in with them.

"You may use mine." Aberto moved forward with a smartphone in his hand.

"Seriously? You have a phone? Does it even work in the dreaming? Who's your carrier?" I was near full-on laughter by the time I was finished spouting off questions. Once again, my sense of self-preservation had kicked in, causing me to find humor in things that shouldn't be funny.

Aberto responded by handing me the phone and rolling his eyes. "Make the calls."

I stared at the phone momentarily, trying to remember the numbers. Pulling myself back from near mania, the numbers finally came back to my mind. I entered them in, hoping beyond hope that Damali would answer.

"Hello?" Damali's voice sounded unsure.

"Damali. It's Izzy. I wanted to let you know that we have uncovered what the darkness is and to ask if you might be able to help with what's coming." The only sound on the other end of the call was a sharp intake of breath that I would have easily missed had I not been paying close attention.

"What is it you think is coming, dear?" The condescension practically dripped from her every word.

"Sonneillon." I wanted to see if she knew who or what it was before I said more.

"You are obviously ill-equipped to be in the position that Isadora left you. Sonneillon is a myth, a story, a demon. I will be no part of whatever this is. I believe you seek to find approval and attention through these dramatic acts. Once you have real evidence of what is coming, then you may call me again." With that, the call was ended.

"Well, looks like she isn't going to be much help. She didn't even believe me." I stared at the phone in disbelief. That woman had promised me just a few days before to help me in any way she could and now she just dismissed me.

"You still have one more Seer to address." Conall's calm voice broke through my thoughts and brought me back to reality.

"Yeah, flighty Francesca is probably going to be a TON of help," Molly quipped.

"I have to try. I promised to keep them informed. Maybe she will surprise us," I supplied, hopefully. "Here goes nothing."

I picked up the phone to dial Francesca's number, when the phone began ringing in my hand. I held it out for Aberto to answer.

"She needs to come NOW!" I heard a voice shout through the phone. "Oh, and in person. No more soul travel!"

"It seems your presence is required by the Order. Are you willing to oblige them?" Aberto asked.

I looked over at Kennan who gave me the "It's up to you" look.

"Only if everyone in this room comes as well." Ian had a lot of built up resentment toward these people and I wanted to find out why. What better way to figure it out than to have him there?

"Not a chance, Izzy. There is a lot that I will do for you, but don't ask this." Ian turned and walked from the room not waiting for a response. So much for that theory. Looked like he wouldn't be mending any emotional fences any time soon. "What about you, you staying or going?" I asked Molly.

"You know he won't let me go if he doesn't, and I won't push him on this. I want to be there with you, but I can't. Looks like the four of you will be handling this on your own." Molly wrapped her arms around me, pulling me close. "Promise me you will be careful, don't do anything reckless."

"I promise that I will try not to do anything reckless." I squeezed her tightly, not wanting to let her go. As I pulled away, she left the room, unable to look back. I sighed, trying to pull my thoughts back to the present.

"I still need to call Francesca, even if we are going to the nut house again. I have to see what she says."

Aberto handed the phone back to me after ending his call with what I could only assume was Sena. She seemed to be my aunt's right hand woman. Or maybe she was her personal assistant. I had no idea how their whole system worked. Looking down at the phone in my hand, my hope was that this call went better than the last had.

"Yes?" Francesca answered.

"Hi, Francesca. This is Izzy." She interrupted me before I was even able to utter the rest of my greeting.

"Please do not think that I will believe this nonsense any more than Damali did. We shall not stand with you on this. Not until you are able to

93

provide irrefutable proof that such a thing could occur. Until then, let me assure you that I am doing all that I can to look into the runes and prophecy to see how they are tied together. Feel free to contact me when you have more substantive evidence." Then it was nothing but the dial tone.

"I mean, I thought they were pissed about me being left in charge, but this is just ridiculous. They said they would help." I stared in disbelief at the phone that had been hung up on me twice as it started to ring once more. I didn't think, I just answered. "Hello?"

"Why aren't you on your way? If you'd left after the last call you could have saved a heck of a lot of time. For craps sake woman, hop to it. Mona is waiting for you. Are you coming or not?" Sena's voice blared in my ear.

"Yes, on our way now. One question. Who is Mona?"

"Your aunt. Now get here, and fast. Some of the Seers had a vision."

"We will get there as soon as we can," I promised.

"I'll make our travel arrangements," Kennan said from the shadows. I really missed the days where he was my teammate and equal. Now it felt like I led a dictatorship. I supposed I was being a bit hypocritical though. It was only two months ago that I was begging the man to treat me like the new Council leader.

"I'll go up and pack our bags. Are you okay to come with us, Conall?"

"As I have told you a thousand times, where you go, I will follow. I will not fail my mother in this, nor will I allow what happened to Cait to happen to you." A haunted look lingered in his eyes. "Now go and pack, I will help Kennan make the arrangements.

Aberto, would you please accompany Izzy so that she is not left alone?"

"I will." Aberto motioned for me to lead the way.

I walked out of the room, pausing to kiss Kennan on his cheek as I went, careful not to let any of the runes touch him, and careful to keep my pukey breath away from him. I was getting downright talented with these acrobatic kisses. I could probably become a contortionist in the circus if this whole Seer thing didn't work out. Because, let's be honest, if it did work out, that meant I had a one way ticket to my demise. I sighed pulling away from Kennan, trying to shake the self-pity off. If it meant keeping that creepy thing from having dominion over the world, I would lay my life down.

"Okie dokie, then. I'll be back down in just a few minutes. Y'all will get everything ready?"

"We will be ready to go when you get back," Kennan assured me. Knowing him, he was calling in the use of a jet of some sort to take us down to Georgia quickly. I wasn't looking forward to that flight.

Chapter Fourteen

I wasted no time gathering my belongings; there wasn't enough time as it was to stop what was coming. Checking the bags once more, I looked over to Aberto and gave a nod. It was time to go, hopefully the Order would have more answers. I walked down the hall from my room, towards the front of the house with Aberto and Conall in tow. I still wasn't sure why both of them needed to accompany me, but arguing would have just taken too much time and quite frankly, more energy than I had to expend.

"Izzy." Molly's hesitant voice pulled me to a stop.

"What is it?" Molly had started to have visions again, and if she looked this concerned, I knew it had to be about that.

"May I speak with you alone for a moment?" She eyed my Guardians warily.

"We don't have much time, but I can make it happen." I shooed Conall and Aberto away. "Just give us a second, would you?"

"We will remain within eyesight, Milady." Conall bowed deeply, moving several steps away.

"Looks like that is as good as it's gonna get. What's up?" I turned my attention back to Molly.

"I don't think you should go, Izzy. I saw something, and I'm not sure what it is, but it isn't good. I don't have a good feeling about any of this. Ian won't be there to watch you and neither will I." Molly's eyes filled with tears as she pulled me against her in a rare show of affection.

Molly, slow down. What did you see? Why are you so worried?" Fear radiated from her body as I held her close.

"I saw the thing come, and I saw, well I'm not sure what they were, but they were fighting the thing, the demon guy. Then I saw you, and you just walked up to it and disappeared." Molly had apparently witnessed what I'd been dreaming for months.

"It's what must be done," I whispered in her ear. "Everything will be alright. Just promise me, that if anything happens to me, you will look out for Kennan. Make sure he is okay." I pulled back to look her in the eyes. I wanted to be sure she understood what I was asking her.

"You better not die, Izzy! I already bought that God awful dress for your wedding." Molly pinned me with her eyes.

"Molly, I will do what must be done. There really is no other option at this point. I'm sorry, but we have to go. Just promise me, okay?" I pleaded, hoping she knew how much I needed this.

"Fine, I promise." Exasperated, she held me with her gaze. "But you better promise me that you won't be ridiculously reckless. You take care of yourself!"

"I promise," I snickered, releasing my hold on her before turning to head down the hall. I couldn't dwell on Molly and Ian staying behind. If what Molly had seen was true, then things were coming much faster than I'd anticipated. I didn't feel ready.

"Are we all set to go?" Kennan's voice pulled me from my thoughts and drew me back to the present. It was time to face the music, or in this case, whatever transportation Kennan had arranged for us.

We walked out into the front of the house, where I expected to see a car waiting. Much to my dismay, out in the open field to the right of the house, a helicopter was landing. So much worse than a plane. How was I supposed to save the world if the very thought of climbing into that thing sent me into conniptions?

"Are you well?" Aberto asked from my elbow.

"Yeah, just peachy," I squeaked as I made my way towards the flying bug. The rickety thing didn't look equipped to carry all of us. Good thing I'd packed light.

Steeling my nerves, I climbed up into the helicopter whispering a prayer for safety as I lowered myself into the seat. No way was I going out in a helicopter crash, it just wouldn't be right.

"Is everyone here?" the unmistakably Guardian pilot asked.

"We're ready," Kennan replied as he climbed in behind me and secured my harness.

I turned my concentration away from my nerves and instead focused on the pilot. I'd seen him somewhere before. I had that stupid tickling sensation in the back of my mind. As his features sank in, I realized he'd been at the warehouse. Obviously, he was a member of the Division.

"It's nice to see you again, Milady," he said.

"You as well...." I was hoping the pause would be enough to get him to supply his name, but no such luck. Secretive Guardian types, they never divulged more information than they thought was needed. Whatever, as long as he could fly the helicopter, I was a happy girl. Well, not a paralyzed with fear girl.

"We should reach the coordinates the Old One provided in about two hours or so, depending on the weather." With that, the pilot started up the helicopter and we were on our way.

"When was the last time you ate?" Kennan, in all of his brilliance, pulled my attention away from the disappearing ground.

"Um, would it be bad if I said I don't remember?"

"It would be normal for you, unfortunately. Which is why I always come prepared." Kennan pulled a bag of sandwiches from below his seat and handed them out to everyone but Aberto. I looked at him but he just shook his head as if it weren't an issue.

"Why didn't you bring him one?" I asked around a bite of brilliant turkey and cheese. It was a good thing my Guardian was such a boy scout.

"He doesn't eat, Izzy. At least he doesn't need to eat to survive," Kennan said in a hushed tone.

"It is no secret, Guardian. I am not ashamed of what I am. I am no longer mortal, Izzy. It has been a very long time since I required sustenance to survive. My mortal form, or shell if you will, perished long ago. I exist in spirit form alone."

"Wait, are you a ghost?" I asked with wide eyes. "Abe the friendly ghost." Okay, the altitude was probably going to my head. Yep, going to blame my diarrhea of the mouth on the thin air.

"I am not a ghost, Izzy." Aberto sighed his deep "I'm irritated with you, you petulant brat" sigh.

"But, you just said you don't have a mortal form. That sort of makes you a ghost." I tried to be all nonchalant, knowing good and well I was driving him insane.

"Do you remember the Seers that were trapped between planes?" Aberto stared out the window of the helicopter off into the distance.

"I don't think I will be forgetting them anytime soon, Aberto," I said as low as I could. The thrumming of the rotors was so loud, I practically had to shout most everything.

"I am similar to them. Only, I am trapped between this realm and that of the dreaming and visions. I am prevented from moving on to what lies beyond the veil." Aberto turned toward me, a look of longing briefly danced in his eyes before disappearing altogether.

"So, not a ghost then?" I sighed, turning my sole attention to more important matters, my sandwich. I reveled in my minor victory, having finally gotten a rise out of Aberto. Lately he'd been so nice to me, I was beginning to worry. Other than his outburst calling me a self-pitying brat, he'd been super supportive. It was freaking me out.

"You shouldn't try to get a rise out of him, Izzy," Kennan admonished, with a crooked smile that ruined any lesson I might've learned.

"He deserves it," I shrugged. It was nice to temporarily take my mind off of things.

I inhaled the rest of my sandwich and settled back into the uncomfortable seat of what must've been a decommissioned military helicopter. Slumping over so that I could use Kennan as a pillow, sleep pulled me in.

Oh great, it was this one again. Talking to Molly must have triggered it. I looked around me as the battle raged in the sky. Darkness and light collided, sending sparks shimmering in all directions. It was the never ending war of the gods, or God, I was getting tired of trying to keep up. Maybe there was a delegation? A panel of gods with a leader sort of situation. I sucked up my apprehension and moved through the clouds. I knew that my demise awaited me, there was no sense in lingering in the clouds longer than need be.

I dropped down to the ground where Sonneillon stood, blackening the earth beneath his feet. This wasn't what I'd seen before. This was different, something was wrong. Surrounding the demon were a vast army of monsters. Nothing made sense as the battle raged. Surely, this was a mistake.

I stared in amazement as the monsters battled. A giant with rage filled eyes relentlessly attacked Sonneillon, repeatedly receiving blows that shook the earth but never once wavering in its resolve. Wolves circled the demon, except they were unlike any wolves I'd ever seen. These looked like they'd been jacked up on steroids and energy drinks. They moved fluidly, ripping into Sonneillon's flesh violently. There were creatures that seemed to sift through the air, disappearing and reappearing in another space within seconds as if they were made of the wind itself. There were so many that my mind could not seem to focus enough to categorize them all.

Surely, this wasn't a vision. Maybe the turkey in my sandwich had been bad. That was it, I'd eaten bad turkey. Which, ultimately, had caused me to have a trippy dream. The vision shifted, revealing the giant to be Kennan and the wolf to be Conall. Definitely bad turkey. I shook my head at the absurdity of it all and trudged on.

The vision wouldn't be complete without the me dying bit. Moving past the crowd of monsters, I looked the demon in the eyes. Approaching it slowly, I tried to remember what needed to be done. I reached my arms out to embrace the demon as I had so many times before. Only, this time as my arms encircled the gargantuan beast, nothing happened. No flash of calm, no disappearing demon, nothing.

"I shall rise," The demon's hot breath promised against my hair. "The Seer shall fall."

The helicopter bounced, pulling me from my bizarre dream. Nothing in it had made sense. I looked over to find Aberto staring at me, concern etching deep lines in his brow. Something in my stomach flipped and I wondered if my turkey had been fine after all. Stupid, inexplicably improbable, visions.

Chapter Fifteen

Luckily the flight only lasted a little over an hour. As we passed above the murky waters of Okeefenokee swamp, I wondered where the pilot planned to set us down. From the looks of things, we may have to rappel out of the stupid thing, which I was so not down for.

"Hold on tight. This might get a bit dicey," The pilot muttered. It was the equivalent of a tattoo artist yelling "Oops" as he worked, not cool at all. I gripped the seat so tightly my knuckles threatened to break through the skin.

The helicopter dropped and rose in minute increments sending my stomach into conniptions. Finally, the earth rose up to meet us and the helicopter stilled upon what I surmised to be the only available hard patch of ground in the entire swamp.

Everything shut off quickly as the pilot instructed us to get our stuff and get out. Much to his chagrin, I was still clinging to the chair like some sort of deranged spider monkey, afraid that if I let go, the helicopter might just fall over.

"Izzy, we've landed. You can get off now," Kennan snickered, trying to pry me loose.

"What?" I looked around trying to gain my bearings. "Oh, right, we aren't dead. Awesome." I still hadn't been able to shake that stupid vision, and the bumpy landing had done nothing to calm my nerves. Now, I had to face my aunt and that completely mental sidekick of hers, Sena.

"It took you long enough to get here. Do you know how long the Grand Seer has been waiting?" I wondered if just thinking of Sena had summoned her from the swamp's murky waters.

"Well, you did say in person. We were in Illinois. Travel takes time," I grumbled, slinging my backpack over my shoulders.

"Fine, excuses later. Let's get a move on." She barely paused to see if we were following before making her way down a narrow boardwalk through the swamp. I looked out at the still waters with trepidation. The probability of getting eaten by gators and being unable to fulfill the prophecy was uncomfortably high.

I started to follow her, but caught Conall in my periphery staring at her, aghast. I'd only seen that look on one Guardian before, and I knew exactly what it meant. Conall had just found his Seer.

"Really?" I sighed. "Her? It couldn't have been a tame, mild-mannered sort?" I huffed, grabbing his hand to pull him in my wake. I had no time for these shenanigans.

"I can't belong to someone in the Order, Izzy. Something must be wrong," Conall whispered as he dropped my hand. He continued to follow me with a look of terror on his face.

"The universe is a mysterious place," Kennan muttered, leading the way behind Sena.

When we finally arrived, after what seemed like miles of hiking through swamp, I finally got a good look at the house I had previously visited in spirit. The house was some strange hybrid of cabin and plantation home that had been weathered. Grayed wood rose up out of the swamp on a peninsula that looked ready to sink into the water at any moment. The rusted tin roof would surely crumble at the slightest touch. I wondered how a bird hadn't just fallen through upon landing, yet. Even with its dilapidated exterior, the house was a bizarrely beautiful place. The ruin had a life, and that life spoke to something deep within me. If there was ever a haunted house, this one would be it.

"Hey, Aberto, when we walk in, can you say 'Boo'?" I was sticking with the whole Aberto was a ghost train of reasoning. Sena snickered, making me like her instantly. Maybe she wouldn't be so bad after all.

"I will not," Aberto muttered, passing me without a spared glance.

"Well, just ruin all of my fun."

"One of these days, he is going to turn you into a frog, Red," Kennan snickered, bending to kiss me on the head.

"Can he really do that?" I asked with wide eyes, to which Kennan shrugged.

"Keep messing with him, and you may just find out." He smiled his half smile before disappearing into the should-be haunted, swamp house.

I followed reluctantly, worried that I might begin sprouting warts at any moment. At least I was in the swamp, frogs liked the swamp. I heard a holler for everyone to move out of the way as we entered the house. It seemed my alleged aunt had been told of our arrival.

"Finally! We need to talk, niece." She didn't hesitate, grabbing my arm and pulling me behind her swiftly.

"Okay, maybe a little slower?" I was struggling to keep up with her long strides up the stairs to her room. The house seemed vastly different than the last time I'd been there. The colors were somehow brighter, and the smells were more prominent.

"We have no time for slow, it is coming, and fast. You must prepare or perish. Those are your choices. If you wish to blindly fall into the whole "Prophecy chosen one" thing, then so be it. But, I made your momma a promise, and I intend to keep it." This woman was a whole ball of crazy if she thought we could stop the prophecy.

Where my mother had been calm, serene, and well-put together, this woman was a hot mess. She was buzzing with frenetic energy that seemed to bounce and zap around her as she moved. It was as if my mother and aunt were balancing the different ends of the spectrum. It made me wonder if my mother's death had thrown off the balance somehow.

"Of course it did, my dear." 'd always wanted a crazy aunt. I guess I should've been more careful what I wished for.

"Please don't do that, or if you do eavesdrop, just pretend you aren't. It creeps me out." I flopped into the first chair I saw once we entered the room. The near crash of the helicopter, fine the landing, and the hike had done me in.

"Oh, sorry. I forget sometimes. I'm sure you know how it is. After two hundred years, things can get a bit fuzzy. Well, of course you don't know the two hundred years part. I'm rambling, aren't I?" She smoothed her dress down, lowering herself into a chair directly in front of me.

"What should I call you?" I had yet to figure out the woman's name, and calling her Grand Seer seemed a bit too formal for family.

"Mona. That's what your mother called me." She smiled brightly.

"Is Mona your name?" The way she'd phrased it confused me.

"No. I honestly don't remember what my given name was. When we were young, your mom used to call me Moan-a all of the time. It started after I became a speaker box for the heavens. I would whine and moan about the headaches afterward. So, to take my mind off of the pain, she used to call me sad little Moan-a." She smiled fondly at what I thought a very strange memory.

"Well that wasn't very nice of her." I was confused how a name like that could bring on fond memories.

"No, she was baiting me. You see, I was always the competitive one between the two of us. Your mom knew that if she made it seem like she was the stronger Seer it would drive me to be better, and handle my gifts more efficiently. She was taking care of me, like she always did." She paused looking down at her hands for a moment before looking into my eyes. "What started as a joke, became a constant reminder from my sister that I was strong enough to endure this."

"I miss her." I hadn't thought about my mom much in the last months. I'd been trying to keep my attention on everything but her absence. But now, in the presence of the only living family I had left, the reality came like an unwelcome slap to the face.

"I know, I do too." Mona moved from her seat to engulf me in a familiar hug. "But, we must move forward. Dwelling in the past will do nothing to save us from what is coming. I need you to be a strong girl now. Okay?" She pulled back, leaving her hands on my shoulders to assess me.

"I know. I just haven't thought much about her and seeing you brings it all back to the surface." I wiped my eyes and nodded, grounding myself in the present. If the prophecy was right, I would be seeing her again soon at any rate.

"We need to discuss what I've been seeing." Mona moved back to her seat and stared at me gravely.

Gone was the kind aunt that I'd just seen. The woman sitting before me was a leader, a force to be reckoned with.

"Well, let's get it over with shall we?" I didn't see any point in postponing the inevitable.

"One moment." My aunt closed her eyes and shook out her shoulders, when she began speaking again, it was no longer her words. "Guard yourself Seer, the darkness shall arise soon. Look not for answers in the fog, for they lie within you. There are enemies at your gates, trust not what you see, but what you feel. The time has come for you to pay the price for the gifts that have been bestowed. Fail and all of your struggles will be for naught."

It would be super awesome if the Big Guy would just give me a simple road map instead of sending me riddles that were impossible to decipher. Or better yet, not just telling me what I already knew. And the whole bit about me paying for the gifts, it wasn't like I'd asked to be born a Seer. As far as I was concerned they could just take their gifts back.

"What am I meant to do? Why won't you just tell me who you are and be done with it?"

"You are meant to fulfill the prophecy. That is both your blessing and curse. As for who I am, when the time comes, all shall be revealed." And just like that my aunt was back to herself, mumbling curses about being used as a loudspeaker. The name Mona was beginning to make more sense.

"Well, did you get anything useful?" My aunt asked.

"Just more riddles, like always," I yawned loudly, trying to suppress my exhaustion.

"Let's find you somewhere to sleep. I won't have my niece falling over from exhaustion. That just won't do!" My aunt got up from her seat, leading me half-asleep, to the door.

"What did you find out?" Kennan asked as we exited the room.

"I found out that the people running the heavens are even more elusive than you lot. So, pretty much, a whole lot of nothing."

"Are you telling me that we have journeyed all this way for nothing?" Aberto's incredulous voice brought more of my attention back to my surroundings.

"I'm not sure yet. Honestly, I'm so tired I could fall over right now. So, my suggestion is that I get some sleep, and maybe just maybe I will have some answers in the morning."

"You and your Guardian can use this room. Conall and Aberto may share the room next to that. These rooms are reserved for our visitors. Sena will answer any questions you may have." With that, my aunt disappeared back into her room to be replaced by Sena.

"Alright, let's get you interlopers settled, shall we?" Sena opened the door to Conall and Aberto's room, gesturing for them to enter.

"Sena, is there a place where we may discuss something privately?" Conall looked nervous as he addressed her.

"Not a chance, dog boy. You Council lot are always trying to stir up trouble. So, get this in your head real quick like, it ain't happening." She eyed him steadily as if he had just propositioned her to give up her maidenhood. "Now, go on in and get Abe settled, he looks a bit restless."

"I did not mean..." Conall trailed off, completely confounded by Sena's response.

"Whatever. In with you. I've got other business to handle and you are wasting my time." Sena turned her attention to us as a befuddled Conall disappeared into the room. "As for the two of you, you will be here."

"Why did you call him dog boy?" Out of everything she'd said that one had stuck with me. It brought me back to the bizarre vision I'd seen on the plane.

"You don't know? Oh, this is going to be a riot when you figure it out. Priceless." She was near the point of hysterical laughter. "In with you now, go on. I'll explain everything later, if your Guardian lets me."

I walked into the sparsely furnished room, with what I was sure was a similar expression to Conall's, utter confusion. My exhaustion pulled at me, there was no way I would be able to think about anything else. I needed to sleep, and quickly. Before Kennan could even utter a word, I collapsed to the floor, never making it to the bed.

Chapter Sixteen

Apparently my protection marks were no longer doing me a lick of good. I could feel him in the fog, the bringer of the darkness. I'd been summoned yet again, and I knew when I awoke I would have another mark. I hoped that I would at least be able to find out who was behind the marks. Perhaps then I would have a better chance of stopping what was coming.

"That would be a helpful bit of information, would it not?" The robed figure emerged from the fog with a grotesque monster following in his wake. The demon was in the dreaming, which meant it was even closer to reality. I watched it flicker in and out of existence; there and gone again. Never settling on this plane completely. It made me nauseous, as if I were staring straight at a strobe light.

I swallowed deeply, fighting the nausea. Tired of the games, the mystery, I ran full-force toward the robed figure. Enough was enough. I used every ounce of the power that I'd gotten from Aberto to make it to him in time to rip his hood down.

His hand shot out sending me flying backwards to land painfully on my back. The man moved to stand over me, a snarl gracing his ruined face. A crescent shape scar dissected his eyebrow and extended downward to culminate at the corner of his mouth, turning the corner up in a constant sneer. Surrounding the scar were a network of spider web-like scars. Lowering himself, he pinned my stomach down with a knee, simultaneously encircling my neck with an iron grip, threatening to cut off my life.

"You should be grateful that we need you to form this bridge. Otherwise, I would have ended you long ago."

I tried to fight the tears flowing down my cheeks as he pulled a stylus out and began to dig deeply into my arm, forming one of the last runes. I thought of Aberto and wished more than anything that he could be there, to somehow protect me from this man they way he'd protected me from my bad dreams. Just as the robed man finished up the mark, Aberto appeared.

A bright light shone as the man was thrown from me in a force unlike any I'd ever seen. Aberto moved toward the fallen man, paying no heed to either me or the demon.

I looked upon the solidified demon. One more mark- that was all it would take for it to break through to the corporeal plane. The smell of the demon's charred skin coated my nostrils as I looked up and up in abject terror. I was frozen, unable to move as it lumbered toward me.

"It cannot be stopped." The demon's voice, like metal grating against metal, sounded in my mind. Hate and fear welled up inside of me instantaneously, causing my stomach to roil. I struggled to find air as the voice echoed through my mind, bringing forth the visions of the burning city and the man with blackened eyes.

I swallowed down my fear, pushing it aside to stand on shaky legs. I turned my attention toward Aberto, no longer able to stomach the demon. Aberto moved towards the sprawled man, a brilliant blue glow surrounding his body. The look in Aberto's eyes terrified me.

"Hello, brother," the man sneered. Betrayal and shock quickly replaced the anger upon Aberto's face.

"It cannot be. Why? Why would you do this? Why bring this destruction down upon the earth we were sworn to protect? We are not meant to interfere! Do you not understand the penalty for what you do?"

"Nothing could be worse than this accursed existence," the man snarled. "Had I acted all those years ago, perhaps I would not be here now. I will bring this world to justice, the justice it deserves. No longer will I protect these undeserving people. Instead, I will make them earn their forgiveness, earn their place in the heavens. The darkness will come and it will purge the earth. Nothing can stop it." He disappeared into the fog with the demon, his words left to echo through the emptiness.

Aberto turned and came towards me slowly, a look of dismay upon his face.

"You came," I croaked. My throat felt bruised from where I'd been held down.

"I will always come." Aberto reached his hand out to help me to my feet.

"Who was he?"

"He is Emmanuel. He is an Old One." Apparently, that was all Aberto would be divulging. With the shock of it all, I wasn't interested in pressing. All I wanted to do was sleep, to actually sleep and rest for more than five minutes.

"Can you help me sleep?"

"I can." Aberto placed his hands on either side of my face to whisper a binding that would prevent me from dreaming, but allow me to rest.

Thankfully, all that remained was the beautiful oblivion.

Being pulled from sleep by Kennan's voice startled me. I felt like I hadn't slept at all and my throat and arm felt as though I had been beaten. Oh yeah, I had. I tried to sit up but fell back against the pillows abruptly.

"Izzy, hold still. The Grand Seer is trying to treat your rune." Kennan pushed gently against my shoulders to hold me in place.

"Which one was it this time? Which rune?" My voice came out a strained rasp.

"It is Kalc," my aunt muttered, doing her best not to touch my skin directly.

I was so tired of being unable to touch anyone but Aberto. It had been months since I'd been able to have my naughty way with Kennan. I missed him. I missed his touch. If anything, I wanted to end all of this just so that I could get laid again. Was that so wrong?

"What's it mean?" I whispered.

"It roughly translates to chalice or offerings." She paused for a moment, finishing up my bandage, "There, all finished. Now, we should get you some food. I will have it brought here because you don't seem exactly mobile at the moment."

"Thank you." I grabbed her hand and squeezed tightly before she left the room.

"What happened in the dreaming? Aberto came back furious and then disappeared once he saw you were safe." Kennan gently stroked my forehead, careful to avoid contact with any of my other skin.

"Aberto knows the man orchestrating whatever this is. He's an Old One, Kennan." My throat felt as though it were lit by fire. I honestly didn't think I would be able to talk much more.

"Explain this." Kennan pointed toward my neck and what I was sure was a gnarly bruise.

"I foolishly tried to figure out who we are up against. He didn't like being unmasked." Swallowing back any further words, I winced.

"Just rest. If you can bring Aberto back, that would probably be a good thing. We need to know what he knows." Kennan rose to his feet and walked to the other side of the room to lean against the dresser. I could see the tension rippling through his back as he stood there. He knew that time was running out, and he was doing everything he could to hide his concern.

"We are going to make it," I promised, as much for myself as for him. I needed to hope that the prophecy could be rewritten.

"You better be right. I can't do this without you, Red. You've been my life longer than I can remember. No more dying, no more risky stunts, no more rushing into the fray. Got it?" Kennan returned to sit next to me on the bed as the door opened.

"I have some grub for you." Sena came in and stopped wide-eyed. "Holy crap! What happened to your neck? Is he beating you? Because, I'll totally kick his ass if he is." She nodded toward an incredulous Kennan.

"Happened in the dreaming," I wheezed.

"Ah, so they pulled ya back in again. Do you mind if I take a look at your protection marks?" Sena moved towards me, setting the food down on the dresser as she came.

"Umm, no?" It didn't seem wise to argue with her at any rate. She was the sort to just plow on through without a second thought.

I sat up slowly, lifting my shirt so that she could see my marks.

"Well, if those aren't working, then nothing will. Does Abe know they aren't working?"

I nodded, afraid to speak much more.

"Hmm, fat lot of good his skills are doing for you. Well, eat up. If what they say is true, this could be one of your last meals." She paused for a moment, surprised by her own words. "Oh, I am so sorry, that was so rude. Sometimes I just don't have a filter. Everything that passes through my head comes out of my mouth. Just forget what I said. We are going to try and do everything we can to keep you safe. Yeah, well. I'm gonna go now." She rushed from the room causing me to snicker.

"She's interesting," Kennan muttered.

I nodded in agreement, doing my best to inch my way towards the food, only to be pushed down by Kennan.

"I'll get it. You just save your energy. Who knows what random acts of insanity you will need to perform today." He smiled brightly as he brought my food over. "After breakfast, you need to get Aberto here. We need to figure out what we're going to do. I can't just sit around any longer, Izzy. We need to do something."

"I know," I rasped. My throat was starting to feel better already, which brought a whole new concern to the foreground. If that was another change, then would I end up like Aberto? He could heal quickly, and if I were starting to heal like him did that mean that I would also end up stuck in between planes for the rest of forever? Terrified by the prospect of spending an eternity neither here nor there, I decided to turn my attention to something else. No sense in worrying about something that hadn't even happened yet.

"Well, eat now, and we'll get everyone together to figure this out." Kennan rubbed his hand down his face heading out of the room. Presumably, to gather everyone to formulate some sort of plan.

I looked around the empty room and wondered how we were ever going to cram everyone in here. I wished that there was some way for me to heal the runes, the way my throat was healing. I brushed off the self-pity and delved into my food. Thank God it was something soft and familiar, grits. I shoveled them down thinking of Aberto, and his reaction to Emmanuel. Things had just taken a giant turn for the worse and I knew it. Whatever came next was going to be a whole heaping ton of suck.

Chapter Seventeen

"I should not have abandoned you. Forgive me?" Aberto appeared in my room before anyone else was able to return, startling me from my food reverie.

"Bells!" I rasped, startled.

"What?" Aberto's eyebrows furrowed in confusion.

"You need to wear them." I gave him a stern look before returning my attention to my deliciously buttery grits.

"Is your throat not healing?" Aberto never would dignify my bells idea with a response. One of these days I was going to buy him one of those jingle bell anklets and strap it on him when he was unaware.

"It feels better than it did when I woke up," I supplied between bites.

"Perhaps your being unable to speak will work to our advantage. I may just be able to get through my story without your interrupting with a thousand unimportant questions." Aberto gave me one of his rare half-smiles as he lowered into the chair closest to the bed. My arm acted of its own accord to smack him.

"Ha. Ha," I wheezed. I figured sign language was probably going to be our best means of communication so I motioned for him to continue.

"Emmanuel is one of the Old Ones, the first of our kind. I knew years ago that he had taken it into his head to bring forth a darkness, but he only had the help of some inferior Guardians and Seers. Ultimately, Cait was able to undo his bindings by sacrificing herself for the sake of those she loved. Emmanuel disappeared after that. All that knew he'd been there had assumed that the gods had finally taken him under their judgment." Aberto dropped his head into his hands. "I didn't know, Izzy. I had no way of knowing that he had survived and still plotted to bring about this ridiculous scheme. Why did the gods not punish him for his acts? Why has he been left to do his bidding?" Aberto looked at me, pain lacing his eyes.

"Because all things have their time, dear one." Mona entered the room so quietly, neither of us had noticed her entrance.

"Is this from you, or them?" Aberto asked, distain dripping from every word.

"From experience. Do you not remember uttering those words yourself to my dear niece? All things have a season, do not lose your faith. If you cannot believe enough to stand, then we shall all fall." My aunt rested a hand on his shoulder before turning back to me. "As for you, let's get you propped up and a bit more presentable, shall we?"

She moved toward me and pulled me up to rest more comfortably against the pillows. I was starting to feel like an invalid. After getting me resettled, she grabbed a makeup remover cloth from my bag and set out to clean my mascara stained face. I didn't even remember putting it on in the first place.

"There now, much better." She left her hand resting on my cheek, the same way my mother had. Tears sprung in my eyes. I was grateful to have something of my mother back. Even if she wasn't my mother, she was my blood.

I nodded as the rest of the group filed in. Conall tried to move next to Sena, who abruptly shot across the room to stand next to my aunt. I'd thought Ian had trouble with Molly. It appeared Conall was in for way more trouble than even Ian had faced. It served him right to get someone as sassy as her though. Maybe she would make him less serious.

"We need to discuss what our next step will be. Now that Izzy only has one mark left before the bridge is complete, we must formulate a plan." Kennan addressed the group with the same military efficiency that he'd used at the warehouse.

"Emmanuel is orchestrating it," Aberto supplied.

"I thought he'd been dealt with. Was he not the cause of the scourge all those years ago?" Conall's anger radiated throughout the room.

"He disappeared. None of us knew he was still walking this plane. I assure you, we had no knowledge of his survival," Aberto pledged.

"If it didn't work last time, why is he doing it again?" I wheezed.

"Rest your voice, Izzy," everyone admonished. Sheesh, you would think a girl asked too many questions or something.

"Something is different this time." Aberto rubbed his hand through his hair, mulling over what could be happening.

"Do you think someone is helping him?" Kennan pinned Aberto with his gaze.

"I do. The question remains, who?" Aberto supplied. "Whomever they are, they are far more powerful than the allies he amassed during his last attempt. These people have power."

"So, what can we do if we don't know who is behind it?" Sena questioned. I was glad that someone else was there to ask, since I wasn't allowed to talk. I gave Sena a quick smile to thank her for doing the job of asking a gazillion questions for me.

"We can prepare," Conall supplied.

"Oh really, dog boy? How exactly do you expect to prepare if you don't even know where they are going to attack?" Sena crossed her arms and eyed Conall who traced across the room quickly to stand over her. "You better not start peeing all over my stuff, mister," Sena muttered, looking up into Conall's face defiantly.

"You will no longer call me that wretched name. Are we understood?" Conall's voice came through gritted teeth. He looked down at her with anger and amazement.

"Fine. But I'm serious about the peeing on my stuff. You better not do it," Sena huffed, nonplussed by Conall's anger.

"Why is she calling him a dog?" I whispered to Kennan.

"Umm, well," Kennan paused, trying to avoid the truth.

"It is time that she knows the truth, Guardian," Aberto said calmly. He was completely unaffected by the chaos erupting in the room around him.

"There is something that we can do, an ancient magic that calls back to our beginnings." Kennan paused trying to find the right words. "You know how you have been manifesting new talents since Aberto breathed part of his soul into you? Well, there is a sort of marking that can call forth our ancient talents. Talents that were repressed for a reason. If a battle is coming, it is one way we can prepare to take on the demon."

"So, what are you saying? Does Conall turn into a collie or something?" My voice was finally starting to sound a modicum of normal.

"I am not a lap dog, Izzy." Conall glared at me as he moved away from Sena to retake his spot across the room. "Our talents are associated with our names. We were given specific names upon birth for this reason."

"So what is your talent? What does your name mean?" I asked Kennan.

"Do you remember when I asked you not to be scared by what you saw in the visions of Cait? I was afraid you would see what I turned into."

"What do you turn into? Stop stalling."

"My name means ancient. One of the earliest gifts bestowed upon our kind, if you wish to call it that, is the gift of unhinged rage. Some have called us berserkers. I morph and change into a rage filled, mindless creature."

"So, you are like the Incredible Hulk?" My eyes were wide. I wondered if he turned green and yelled "Hulk Smash."

"Yes, but without the green. And no, I don't say Kennan Smash." He knew me too well.

"So, what about you?" I asked Conall.

"My name means strong wolf," Conall supplied.

I started laughing uncontrollably. Suddenly, Sena's comments about dog boy and peeing on her stuff made a whole lot more sense. Then I got the image of a wolf wearing an eye patch in my head and there was no coming back.

"I think that she's finally cracked, brother," Conall muttered to Kennan.

"Just give her a moment."

"Do you still wear the eye patch when you are all wolfed out? Please tell me that you do. Oh, are you like a werewolf? Do full moons make you want to chase your tail?"

"I'm not a werewolf. Have you not listened to anything, woman? I become a wolf in the same way that Kennan morphs into a berserker. It is a repressed, or dormant, talent. So no, I don't chase my tail at the full moon, and no I don't wear my eye patch in wolf form." Conall didn't seem to find the situation as funny as I did. I couldn't understand how he didn't find it at least a little bit amusing. A dog with an eye patch, it was funny. I didn't care what he said.

"Sorry," I muttered, only half meaning it. "So, that is the best plan we have? You guys get the gang back together and tap into your old school talents and fight the demon? We don't even know where the durn thing will surface."

"It will surface wherever you are. That is one of the few things working to our advantage," Aberto added.

"Why did you not tell us this when it was Cait's life on the line?" Conall was growing angrier as the moments passed. I'd wondered when this would come up for some time and I was surprised that it had taken so long.

"Her destiny was sealed." Aberto's answer did nothing to subdue Conall.

"As is Izzy's, yet you consistently intercede on her behalf."

"Would you rather I let her die?" Aberto asked calmly.

"That isn't what I mean. I want to know what makes now different than then? What about her makes you step in when it is meant to be forbidden?" Conall got dangerously close to Aberto, staring up into his face defiantly.

"When the gods speak, I listen. I was given an order to protect Izzy at all costs." Aberto stood to his towering height and looked down at Conall. "Cait knew her destiny was sealed. She had a choice, as does Izzy, to allow the darkness to reign or put an end to it. Do not let her sacrifice be in vain. Do not allow your petty resentment to cloud your judgment and distract you from today's goal. Yesterday is gone and can never be repeated. Things lost cannot be

returned," Aberto said the last looking at me. I wasn't
sure if he was just looking at me or trying to deliver
another one of his infamous cryptic messages. I'd
given up long ago trying to decipher his hidden
messages. Until he gave me the secret decoder ring, I
was done.

"But why now? Just answer that, satisfy our
curiosity. I'm not the only one that questions your
motives. In a time of treachery, such as this, it is best
to know everyone's intentions." Conall wouldn't let it
go.

"Why now? Because Izzy is important, not just to
this world, but to me. She saved me from a darkness
none of you will ever know and I cannot let that kind
of a gift go ignored. Why her? She is bigger than all of
us, bigger than anything any of us will ever be able to
imagine. Her destiny has been written in the stars
since the dawn of time. Why her? She is the light that
shines brightest when nothing else but darkness
exists. Her light matters, and I will do all in my power
to ensure that it never gets extinguished." Aberto
faded in a cloud of anger, leaving us all staring at
where he'd been moments before. I was pretty sure I
was the only one that Aberto gave long speeches to,
and mostly they were to yell at me to stop being a
baby. He'd just laid down some serious stuff at
everyone's feet and vanished without so much as a
goodbye.

"Well, looks like you pissed Abe off," Sena
supplied.

"Thanks Captain Obvious," Conall huffed,
turning to leave the room. I was so proud, it looked
like I'd rubbed off on him after all. Even if it was just
one phrase, I would get him there eventually.

"What? What did I do this time?" Sena threw her
hands up and fell into the chair that Aberto had

occupied earlier. "I really should get some sort of filter installed up here. Do you think Abe has a marking for that?"

"I have no idea." I smiled at Sena, wondering how I could find someone so socially inept so likeable. Oh, that's right, she reminded me of myself.

"Well now you know why I called him dog boy."

"How did you know that he could do that? I've known these guys for a while now and I had no clue." I looked at her in wonder, there was something so familiar about her.

"Cait was my, wait for it, great aunt. The stories have been passed down through our family about that day. It is really something I need to ask you about, when you have some private time." Sena looked down at her hands, mumbling the last part.

"Well, it seems that this meeting has gone awry, and I can't really get up and leave. So, now works if you've got the time."

"Do you think we may be able to speak privately?" Sena looked around the room at everyone that still lingered.

"You aren't planning to shank me or anything are you?"

"No, if I'd wanted to do that, I already would have."

"Well, that's a comfort." I paused looking over to where Kennan and my aunt were in a deep discussion. He looked up to catch my eyes and moved towards me.

"What is it, Red?" Kennan's eyes were filled with concern, as if I would reject him now that I knew he turned into a big hulking beast.

"Sena needs to talk to me, and she doesn't want to have an audience. Do you think that maybe I can talk to her alone? She promised not to shank me," I provided.

"Sure, I'll be right outside talking with Mona if you need me."

"I love you, big guy. Nothing will ever change that." I reached up and grabbed his hand before he left. Even with the world at stake, he was still the most important thing to me.

Chapter Eighteen

As everyone left the room, I turned my attention back to Sena. She seemed so young, somehow, sitting there in front of me.

"What did you want to talk about?"

"The stories of you."

"Oh, don't believe anything anyone has told you. Or, you know, if it is good then believe that part. Listen, I'm just getting the hang of this whole Seer thing. I don't really know what I'm doing." I was starting to do my whole nervous rambling thing, and I knew it.

"Would you put a sock in it, already? This isn't about the fact that you are fumbling through being a Seer like some sort of drunk person playing pin the tail on the donkey. This is about the stories, the stories of Cait and the message she sent through our family for generations to make sure it got to you."

"Oh! There's a message?"

"Yeah, oh." Sena looked at me impatiently. "I need you to grab my hand. You have to flip through my memories to find it. She said that you would know it when you saw it and to let go and find her."

"But, she was trapped there all those years. She's finally moved on. Won't this just pull her back to this plane?"

"No, this is an echo. She made a permanent recording in our collective memory so that you would know what she knew in the end."

"Just be careful not to touch the runes, okay?" I held my hand out towards Sena, almost afraid of what awaited.

"Are you ready? Focus on Cait, and you should find it pretty quickly."

Sena's cold hand entwined with mine sending me spiraling through her history. Not just her history, but her whole family's collective history. It was the most bizarre thing I'd ever experienced while trying to memory sift.

"Izzy," I heard Cait's voice call out. I stopped sifting and immediately walked toward where she stood on the scorched earth. "It has taken you far longer to find me than I'd hoped."

"Wait, I thought you were just a memory."

"I told them that so they would not fret over me. The gods bid me to tell you of what comes. You can defeat it, if you wish." Cait cocked her head to the side as if questioning whether or not I would stand against the darkness.

"Of course I want to defeat it."

"You misunderstand me. The power to defeat the beast comes from within you. If you believe that you can destroy it, then you will. I believed my sacrifice would stop it, and it did."

"So you are telling me to have faith that I am enough. What if I believe that I can stop it without dying? Will that also happen?"

"All things have a price, Izzy. You must be willing to pay the price for what you seek. The price for the eternal end to this darkness is that you must fall. If you do not, if you fail to do what you are called to do, then the darkness will once more return to reign eternal. You need to look within yourself and find what is most important to you. Is it your life that matters, or the life of those that you love? What are you willing to do to protect them?"

"Everything," I breathed out. "It has to be this way then? I must sacrifice myself to save everyone I love?"

"You must be willing to sacrifice yourself to end the darkness." Thanks cryptic Cait. These people could seriously write books on how to be evasive.

"Is that all you have for me? Believe it and it will happen?" It sounded like some absurd self-affirmation bologna.

"I have one more piece of advice before you go. Try not to let what is coming pull you into the darkness. It is tempting to let it overtake you. You are much stronger than I ever was, you must fight it. If you roll over now, you will never again get up."

"Okay, so drink some water and suck it up. Anything else?"

"Tell Conall to be nice to my Sena. She hasn't had an easy road." Cait smiled softly as reality came crashing back in.

Sena broke contact abruptly, sweat drenched her brow.

"Are you alright? Did I hurt you?" I was worried that I somehow did something wrong. I wasn't exactly an expert at any of this yet.

"I heard everything while you were there. That was the most bizarre thing I've ever been a part of. And what the heck does she mean about Conall being nice to me?" Sena paused for a moment and then her eyes grew as large as saucers. "Oh no! No. No. Just no. This can't be happening. Not dog boy." Sena stood and started pacing the floor. Her hands shaking as she looked up towards the sky. "Really, him? It couldn't have been a nice, normal, Order Guardian?"

"For what it's worth, he isn't that bad. You could always dress him up like a pirate on Halloween. That would be a perk."

"Oh, you've got jokes, do you?" Sena plopped heavily back in the seat, her hands shaking. "Well, what am I supposed to do now? He doesn't even like me, for crying out loud. I always thought I would end up in some romantically charged match like you and Kennan have. Are you telling me that I am cursed to the platonic playground for the rest of my very long life?"

"I'm saying that you probably need to talk to him and figure it out. I wouldn't exactly write it off just yet." I remembered Conall's face when he'd first seen her and I knew, undoubtedly, the feelings brewing beneath the surface were far from platonic. The look he'd given her was definitely not of the familial persuasion.

"Talk. I can talk. Not well, and not with a filter, but I can do it. Now, back to the other parts. How was she there? It was just supposed to be a recording of a memory." Sena pinned me with her gaze, effectively redirecting the conversation.

"My visions are funky. They never are simple." I pulled myself up in the bed doing my best to shake off the exhaustion pulling at me. "I need to get up and get dressed. Can you help me?"

"What, like a nursemaid?"

"Or a friend?" I suddenly missed Molly. Had she been there with me, she'd already have me up and moving to get dressed.

"I think I can handle that." Sena smiled brightly. I wondered just what had happened to her to leave her in such a state. "Are you even up to moving about though? I'm pretty sure your Guardian is going to give me a royal beat down if I come out of this room with you."

"Nah. He is a big old softie. Well, apparently not when he turns into a rage beast, but otherwise we're good. Besides, you heard what she said. If I don't get up and shake off this darkness weighing on me, I will succumb to it. If I let the darkness win then I won't be a whole lot of good to anyone and all of this trouble will be for nothing."

"True. Alright, so are sweatpants and a t-shirt enough? Or are you thinking dressy casual?" Sena hovered over my suitcase, assessing its meager contents.

"Sweatpants. Let's take this whole shaking off the darkness thing one step at a time."

"Okay, then. Up you go." Sena brought some clothes over to me so that I could get dressed.

"Why are the smallest things so hard right now?" I groused.

"Probably because you are marked from head to toe with soul sucking runes," Sena supplied matter-of-factly.

"Do you always state the obvious, or is this just something you do with me?" I asked, wondering if there was a way I could install a filter in the girl's head.

"Nah, I do it with everyone." Sena helped me get dressed, which turned out to be a very slow process. What with the circus acrobatics required to avoid touching my runes and the exhaustion pulling at me with every breath I took. I was surprised we managed it at all.

By the time we'd finished, I was ready to climb straight back into the bed. The only thing that kept me from doing it was Cait's warning ringing in my head. If I wanted to end this, I had to fight what was happening to me.

"Alright, let's go find everyone else. Do you think you can act as my crutch? I'm not so good with the coordination thing on days when I'm not falling to

131

pieces. Which really just means I'm bound to face plant if I don't have someone holding me up right now."

"I gotcha." Sena grabbed my elbow, supporting my weight as we made our way to the door.

Kennan grabbed ahold of me as soon as we made it through the door, helping to steady me.

"Whoa, there. Where exactly do you think you are going?" Kennan raised a brow at me like I'd lost my ever loving mind.

"I'm going to find some answers, to talk to my aunt, and contact the Council members." I eyed him steadily, waiting for an argument. Instead, he clenched his jaw repressing any admonishments he might have wanted to say.

"Okay. At least let me help you get to her rooms." Kennan wrapped his arm under me, half-steadying, half-carrying me as we went.

"Thank God. She is heavy," Sena breathed, shaking out her arm where she'd just been trying to hold me up.

"Thanks a ton, Sena." Hopefully she picked up on the sarcasm.

"Anytime," she smiled brightly before bouncing down the hall and disappearing.

"That girl is strange," I muttered to myself.

"Pot, meet kettle," Kennan replied. Even in my dire state, Kennan still made fun of me. The butt.

"Whatever, just get me to my aunt. I need to talk to her and then contact the Council. Things are coming to a head more quickly than I think any of us anticipated they would."

"We're getting there. Don't be so impatient," Kennan grumbled, practically dragging me down the hall.

Chapter Nineteen

The journey to my aunt's room was treacherous and unforgiving. Okay, so maybe it was the exhaustion speaking, but I hadn't even gone five doors down and I was ready for a nap. The sooner this whole thing was over the better. At this rate, I would probably welcome the end, just so that I could get some rest. I shook myself, remembering Cait's words. If I didn't focus on trying to overcome this, I could very well succumb to the darkness. It was tempting.

"Well, come in. Don't just hover outside of the door like some creepy lurkers." My aunt's voice came from behind her door.

"We're coming. We're just moving a little more slowly than normal," Kennan muttered.

"Why is she out of bed? Why are you out of bed?" She looked to Kennan and then me for answers.

"Because there is no time to rest, and I need some advice. I don't really know what my next step is. I know that I'm supposed to contact the Council and let them know that we have proof. But, aside from that, I'm not really sure what is coming. What do you think I should do? Do the heavens have any messages for me? You know, advice or anything. Maybe a 'How to Defeat Demons: A Step By Step Guide'?"

"Nothing will ever be that simple." My aunt looked at me skeptically.

"Well, that sucks," I huffed, as Kennan helped me to the closest seat. "So, what do you think I should do?"

"I think that you should follow your own instincts. What are they telling you to do?"

"I feel like I need to head back to the Council and call back Damali and Francesca. They need to be involved in this. Even if I don't like them, I could use their help."

"If you do call them back, you must no longer conceal what is happening to you. They must know everything if they are going to help you." Something in my aunt's face shifted and I knew that someone was about to talk through her. She turned toward me fully, and began to speak in her creepy possessed voice. "The truth can no longer be hidden. Reveal your secrets to the Council, for in the revelation more things may be illuminated. Take your Guardian and the Old One but leave Conall. When you return, which you will, bring with you those that you wish to protect."

"What do you mean? I thought the Council was supposed to help me? Why would I be returning?"

"The truth will become clear and you will return to your aunt. You must journey this path if you hope to overcome the darkness."

"Riddles. Why do you people always speak in riddles? Why can't it be 'This is point A, now journey to point B'?" I practically shouted at whomever was currently using my aunt as a voice box.

"The most important things in this life require the greatest commitments and sacrifice. If everything was easy, nothing would be worth the earning," the voice responded sardonically.

Then the possessor faded, whomever he was. I was certain it was a guy, only a man could be that infuriating.

"Okay, so I guess just keep my bed warm then. It looks like I'll be heading back to the Council to discuss this and what is happening to me."

"Are you sure that is wise? Are you sure you are well enough to travel?" Concern radiated from my aunt.

"No, but the big chief seems to think it is a necessary part of my journey," I moaned, bringing my hand to cover my face. "Is there any way to get your friend with the helicopter back here? More importantly, is there an easier way to get back to where that helicopter lands?"

"Of course there is. We just wanted to make sure that you could be trusted before revealing our location. Should you choose to betray us, we would've had time to escape." My aunt's smile was sly.

"Well, no betrayal will come from me. I know how much that sucks. I guess we'd better go tell Conall the plan. I'm sure he will be thrilled. Oh, and call the Council peeps. Order them in for a meeting." I fell back against the chair, slipping into a shallow sleep momentarily.

"Izzy, we need to get going." Kennan lifted me from the chair to be cradled in his arms.

"I can walk," I murmured sleepily.

"Not a chance. Today you don't have to feign strength. Today, you rely on me." Kennan kissed the top of my head and I gave up any fight that I might have had left in me.

"Okay. But I haven't called the Council."

"Eleanor is taking care of it. They should be there when we return. They all live fairly close to the Council headquarters. For now, rest. Save your strength. You are going to need it."

I started thinking about everything that was left to come, and wondered how I would have the strength to get through it. I couldn't even walk myself to a helicopter. I had to be carried. The darkness pulled at me, tempting me with the peaceful oblivion that it would provide if I only let it. There would be no more pain, no more struggle. I could give in. I could just leave this world and everything it contained, behind. I never wanted this fight to begin with.

"Stop it!" Aberto shouted from behind us. I hadn't even seen him come back. "You will not give into this, do you understand me? You are far too strong to let them win."

"What is he talking about, Izzy?" Kennan asked quietly as we approached the waiting helicopter.

"He was putting his nose where it doesn't belong again. Even if he is right, and I do need to fight this." I evil eyed Aberto, trying my best to ignore the fact that he was completely right.

"You didn't answer me. What was going through your mind just now?" Kennan looked down on me, concern etching his face.

"I was thinking of how easy it would be to give in, to surrender to the darkness and just fade away. I'm so tired, Kennan. I'm tired of the fighting, of the running, of the never truly being safe. I'm tired of not knowing who I can truly trust. I'm tired of all of the riddles. I'm just," I sighed heavily, "tired."

"I know, but if you give in, what will become of us?" Kennan knew what I needed to hear to keep me on track. If it was only my life at stake, I would surrender in a nanosecond. But, it wasn't. Everyone was looking to me to end this, to save them. I wouldn't fail them. I wouldn't let them down.

"That is the only thing keeping me grounded," I muttered.

We arrived at the helicopter quickly. I hadn't even noticed the path we'd taken in the midst of my internal misery. We moved toward the helicopter, Kennan gently placing me in the seat. Within a matter of minutes he'd strapped me in tightly and climbed in to sit next to me.

Aberto followed, placing himself so that he could sit directly in front of me. Anger combined with fear masked his face, hiding whatever thoughts he had. I started to ask him what was going through his mind, when he abruptly looked up at me. His eyes were a glowing blue that I'd only seen once, the night he'd pulled Xavier's soul from his body. Something was coming, and he knew what was about to take place. Every fiber of my being screamed to find out.

"I am not at the liberty of answering your questions." Aberto's eyes flamed as he looked back down at his hands. "Believe me, could I forewarn you, I would. Could I prepare you for what you must face, what you must overcome." His voice trailed off, leaving me in a panic. What did he know? Had it been something he'd always known? What was I about to walk into back at the Council? He reached his hand out to engulf mine. "You will endure. You must."

"Is it something you can tell me?" Kennan looked between us, concerned.

"Yes, and I fear I must. You need to know what is coming."

"That is so not fair," I mumbled.

"Izzy, I have broken one of the gods' directives to ensure your safety. I cannot do so again. Please do not ask this of me." His eyes were a slow burning ember, no longer the fire they'd been moments ago.

"Meh, it probably wouldn't help to know at any rate." I let go then, allowing sleep to overtake me. At least I knew I wasn't falling into the dreaming. Instead, where I was going was far worse. It was a parade of memories, of happy times over the years, before I knew what I was. Before this whole destiny business came knocking on my door. It was a cruel reminder of a life that was never real, a life covered in misdirection and deceit all for the greater good.

Chapter Twenty

We arrived back at the Council headquarters far more quickly than I would've liked. I felt an uneasiness sink in as we disembarked the helicopter. At least I was able to walk out on my own two feet. That seemed like a small step forward, even if it was miniscule.

We walked around the house and entered the front doors, which were currently flanked by people from Damali and Francesca's entourage. I had a sinking feeling in the pit of my stomach. Whatever was about to go down, it wasn't going to be pleasant. Instead of heading to the office, I headed up to Molly's room to tell her to get her and Ian's things together.

"Molly?" I knocked on the door, trying not to draw too much attention to myself. "Are you in there?"

"Yeah, what's up?" She opened the door, a strained smile masking her face.

"Giddy-up," I said. We'd decided we needed some sort of 'it is time to jump ship' code after everything that had happened back at the lab. It seemed now would be the first time we actually got to use it.

"Do I need to round up the posse?" Her overly bright smile and wide eyes set my stomach in knots.

"Yes, E and I most definitely need to be brought in. Meet us by the bird in the yard." I looked at her solemnly before turning on my heel to face the people waiting for me in Isadora's old office.

The moment the doors opened, everything stopped. Time seemed to stand still as I approached my desk, where Damali was making herself quite at home. I stood there staring at her. I hadn't put in the contacts. I hadn't masked anything that had changed about me. It was all there for them to see. No more secrets, no more lies. It was time to see the truth. Would they stand with me, or would they be too caught up in their own ascension to the throne to stop the darkness?

"Will you help stop the coming storm? The darkness approaches. Only one mark remains. Will you stand with me?" I stood, grounded in place with Aberto and Kennan just behind me.

"Will we stand with you?" Damali shouted thunderously, rising from her seat. "You who have conspired with the Order behind our backs. You who have withheld evidence from us about Isadora's death. You are not fit to lead us. Look at you, you aren't even a Seer. You are an Abomination."

"So this is how it will be, then? You will turn your back on what Isadora wanted? You will turn your back on the calling to protect this world? This is a directive straight from the heavens, yet you think that you can turn your back and suffer no consequences." The rage boiled up inside of me, causing blue sparks to ripple down my arms. These were supposed to be the people I depended upon, the people I could trust the most. Yet here they were, turning their backs on me when I needed them the most.

"You are an Abomination," Brutus shouted. It looked like I never would find out his real name, not that it mattered. If I stuck around him for too long, my ear drums would just start bleeding, and I'd never hear his name.

"So it is true?" Francesca's small voice cut through the tension. "He did breathe his soul into yours. I'd been told, but until this moment, I did not believe it possible. You truly are no longer a Seer.

Therefore, you are no longer welcome here. You will find no refuge amongst our kind. Anyone that provides you shelter will be given the same punishment - banishment."

There they were, the same words I'd spoken to Elaine only days before, thrown right back in my face. I was being banished, exiled from the family that had taken me in and repaired me after the lab incident. The anger fluxed inside of me, causing my arms to glow an eerie blue. I wasn't sure what would happen if I didn't get my emotions under control.

"Know this, if you turn your back now, there will be a price. The darkness will fall. Stand with me or against me, but there is no middle ground." My voice boomed through the office, fury churned within me.

"Then count us against you." Damali's snide reply caused my anger to arc out, snapping at the desk she stood behind. In an instant, the desk was no more than a pile of ashes. So that's what the lightening did, interesting.

"Izzy, we must go." Aberto gently touched my shoulder pulling me towards the door, as the shocked Council members stood gaping in my direction. "Let go of the anger, or it will consume you." I tried to breathe deeply and let it go.

The Council members stood in shocked silence as we left the room. Exiting the office, angry tears began to drench my cheeks. My home had just been stripped from me, the only place I'd felt like I belonged in a long time. Like Elaine, I'd been banished, never to return again, and all for something that was wholly out of my control. I hadn't asked for this to happen to me.

Numbly, my legs carried me out of the house toward the waiting helicopter. Eleanor, Molly, and Ian were already strapped inside. Curious looks garnered each of their faces.

"What happened?" Molly's voice was strained. Lord only knew what they'd been through the past few hours.

"If you come with me now, you will be banished and no longer recognized by the Council. I can't ask you to do that. If you want to stay, I will understand."

"Screw that. Those bitches just mutinied against my sister's wishes. I'm coming with you. The Order always fascinated me, anyhow," Eleanor piped in, causing me to smile.

"What about you guys?" I asked Ian and Molly.

"We can't go to the Order, but we will stand with you. If you could take us back to Chicago that would be best." Molly held Ian's hand tightly as he let go of a breath.

"Are you sure?" Ian asked her.

"Of course I am. I'm not making you go anywhere you don't want to, at least not unless it is necessary." Molly paused to look back at me, "It isn't necessary we come with you, right?"

"No. I would much prefer that you weren't there when the big bad ugly comes knocking. At least I would have two less people to worry about." I grabbed Molly's hand to squeeze it as the helicopter took off, leaving what had become my home behind. I wondered if I would ever truly have a home again.

"Brother, are you sure my presence is not needed?" Ian asked Kennan gravely.

"You were there the last time, Ian. You know that one more person will not make a difference. The rest of the Division is already on their way to where the Order is currently housed. If something changes, or if something happens, you will need to come." They shared a look that spoke of a thousand secrets shared between them.

"I swear it," Ian pledged, grabbing Kennan's elbow and aligning their forearms as he did. I'd only seen Guardians do this once before, but now looking at it with changed eyes, I saw the magic in the binding.

"Then we need to head to Chicago first," Kennan told the pilot as the helicopter shifted to adjust course.

We rode the entire way in silence. Still stunned by the Council member's reaction, my mind mulled over everything that had transpired. Aberto was keeping secrets, he'd said as much on the way there. I wondered if he'd known what was waiting for me back at the Council, or if his secrets were something altogether different.

"No, Izzy," Aberto said, barely above a whisper.

"But..." I started.

"No," Aberto's eyes flashed a bright blue before dying back to their normal color. Okay, someone hadn't taken his crazy pills. You'd have thought he'd be used to my relentless curiosity by now.

"Fine," I ground my teeth together. I marinated in the events that had just unfolded. I'd been deposed, tossed off the throne, as it were. It stung more than I cared to admit. I knew that I was unfit to lead anyone, but hearing it actually said by someone else was a giant blow to my already frail ego. I thought I'd been doing pretty durn well considering my total lack of experience.

Grappling with what they'd said, my mind reeled. My changes had somehow dubbed me an abomination. Quite frankly, abomination seemed like a strong word. Maybe weirdo, I'd even give them freak, but abomination? Come on. I'd show them abomination. I'd lightning zap their arses. That'd show them.

The helicopter began its decent toward Chicago, and Molly's stop.

"Izzy, we've got to go," Molly pulled me from my thoughts. "I'm sorry I can't come with you. He just isn't ready, and I won't force that on him." Molly seemed torn between being there for me and being with her Guardian.

"He needs you more than I do," I smiled warmly at my friend. "If anything should happen, just know that your friendship has meant more to me than you will ever know. You saved me, and I never really thanked you for that. I love you, Molly. Promise me you will take care of yourself and keep working your fashion rehab magic on Ian?"

"Promise me you won't make any stupid decisions?" Molly's tears matched my own. I knew this very well could be the last time that I saw her bright face.

"I wouldn't be me if I didn't," I snot-laughed. Trying to cover my sobs with a chuckle.

"Don't get dead, Pip Squeak," Ian ruffled my hair as he exited the helicopter.

"See you soon," Molly hugged me tight, not giving a rat's butt that she might touch my runes, and for that, and so many other reasons, I loved her.

"See you soon," I knew it was a promise I wouldn't be able to keep.

Just like that, they were gone and we were lifting off, heading back towards the Order and my inevitable doom.

Chapter Twenty One

An irritating silence prevailed the remainder of the way back to the swamp. An entire two hours filled with nothing but my own misery to keep me company. When the stupid helicopter finally landed and I made my escape, I was ready to scream.

Everything was falling apart and there was no way for me to hold it all together. I was powerless. A chain reaction had begun; as if the fates had set up an intricate path of dominoes to topple, and I was the last one in line. I could see them coming for me, but I could do nothing to prevent my fall. Just as the prophecy had predicted, I would fall. I stood, rooted to the ground just outside of the helicopter, filled with anger.

"I thought it was supposed to be about choice. I thought I had a choice. What happened to that?" I yelled at Aberto. He should know. He was the oldest of us, the wisest.

"Choice is an illusion, Izzy. There is not always going to be an easy choice, or a good one. Sometimes, no matter what you decide, it will not end well. You still have a choice here. You can choose to fight, or you can choose to lay down and let the darkness consume you and everything else in its path. Either way, this is your decision. I hope that you choose not to fall back on your weakness, but to press on. If you don't, everyone you care for, everyone you love, will suffer. Don't be weak," Aberto turned away from me, vanishing as he walked. Don't be weak, the bastard. I'd show him weak when I zapped him with a lightning bolt.

"Izzy, what is this all about?" Eleanor came to my elbow, gently cradling it.

"I feel like there is absolutely nothing I can do to stop this darkness and this demon. All anyone has told me is to believe I can and the power is within me. To me it sounds like a load of affirmation bull crap."

"I might have found something that will help you," Eleanor raised a brow in my direction. "It is, in a word, unconventional. But, if we are lucky, it may just provide you with enough strength to finish this."

"I trust you. If you think it is a good idea, I will give it a go. I don't think things could get much worse as it is." I looked at her, wondering just what I was getting myself into this time. I should really learn to ask more questions.

"Well, I will discuss it with your aunt and see what she thinks when we get there." Eleanor kept her hand on my elbow, guiding me towards the house.

"Wait, you knew she was my aunt? How is it that everyone seems to know everything about me, but no one is willing to tell me anything at all? There needs to be a secret intervention. No more! I swear, how am I supposed to do anything if I don't have all of the necessary information?"

"The Order is not something we are permitted to discuss. I only knew because of your mother. You had chosen the Council, which meant the Order was no longer an option for you," Eleanor said matter-of-factly, as if I were some sort of unruly student.

"I didn't know I had any other option!" I shouted. Exhaustion pulled at me compounding with the elephants practicing their tap routine on my brain. My head would split at any moment, I just knew it.

"That is not my fault. You just didn't ask. If you had, I would've told you," Eleanor looked completely unaffected by my outburst. She reminded me too much of Isadora sometimes.

"Come on, Izzy. We still need to make it back to the house before dark. The last thing we need is for you to be eaten by an alligator. Speaking of food, we need some. I'm starving," Kennan rubbed his belly in mock affront.

"I haven't kept you from food," I mumbled under my breath as we made our way over the boardwalk toward the house.

"Your lack of an appetite interferes with my grazing schedule. So, it sort of is your fault. You confuse me by not eating. It isn't normal." Kennan raised a brow, challenging me.

"Neither are the gluttonous amounts of food you consume, but you don't see me complaining." I needed sleep, I was getting seriously crabby.

"Keep it up and I will toss you to the gators, woman." Kennan swatted my butt, causing me to jump.

"Hey, invalid here. Remember?" I yawned loudly, the adrenaline of the day wearing off as we approached the house. "I think I'm too tired to eat. Can I just sleep instead?"

"No, you need energy." Kennan wouldn't budge on the whole food issue.

"Fine," I grumbled as we approached the house. A chorus of cicadas and tree frogs resounded loudly around me, announcing the coming night. I wondered, as we entered the house, if this would be my last night; if these were the last sounds of the South I would hear before the darkness fell, taking me with it.

"That's enough." Aberto appeared at my elbow, pulling me to a stop. "You will not be able to stop this if you keep succumbing to such morose thoughts. You are not who you were when the prophecy came into existence. I've changed you, therefore there is a chance that the prophecy has also changed. Do not give up this fight so readily."

"Do you think that I want to feel this way, Aberto? This isn't a vacation for me, but you've said it yourself, my choices are all bad. I either lay down now and let it consume me or I fall trying to defeat it. The word fall doesn't exactly give me any hope of survival. I don't have any plans of coming out of this thing intact. Just let me mourn the loss of things, let me deal with this how I must. I'm not as strong as you seem to think I should be. I'm not you, Aberto." Tears streamed down my cheeks as my fear came rushing to the surface. I was barely strong enough to stand on my own two feet, let alone defeat the demon.

Aberto grabbed my shoulders and shook them, making me look him in the eyes. "You are strong enough, do you understand?"

"Just because you wish it to be does not make it so." I turned, and walked into the house where a concerned Kennan was waiting.

"What was that about?" Kennan looked between a furious Aberto and me.

"Nothing important." I walked passed Kennan toward where my aunt and Eleanor were talking.

"So, what's the verdict?" I asked the women.

"The verdict is, you need to eat, and we will discuss her ideas after you have had some sleep. You must rest, Izzy. Do not let yourself get worn down," my aunt admonished.

"But all of this inaction is not doing a durn thing to help me feel like I have any control over what is coming. Everyone keeps telling me to be strong, but just waiting around for this demon to come chomp at me is not my idea of a good time. I'm not hungry, I just want to sleep." The electricity began to flicker down my arms, causing tears to well in my eyes. "And why does this keep happening? I can't even control it. Gah!" I shouted as I made my way towards the room Kennan and I had occupied the night before. I just hoped it was still ours.

Aberto started to move towards me, but Kennan pulled him to a stop. "Give her some time. She needs to be alone right now, otherwise she won't come back to herself. Sometimes we have to let her go." Kennan's last words before I disappeared into the room peaked my interest. "So, perhaps you and I can discuss that secret that you would not divulge in the helicopter."

"Now would suffice," Aberto replied.

I stormed into the room, wallowing in my own misery. The secrets that had brought me to this point swirled around in my mind, pulling me in a thousand directions. I threw myself on the bed, my head spinning, and I couldn't take it any longer. I ripped my soul from my body and ventured out to find Kennan and Aberto. I wanted to know what they were saying. I wanted the truth, for once. Directives be damned, I was so tired of being in the dark.

I turned a corner, searching for them, and came to an abrupt halt when I finally spotted them. They were on the back porch, sitting on the stairs, staring off into the swamp.

"Are you certain?" Kennan's strained voice asked.

"I've known my entire life. I saw it the day I was brought into existence, and I've seen it every day since." Aberto looked off, trying to mask the sadness in his eyes. I knew that if I so much as breathed, I would be caught. I held as still as I could, waiting for what they may say next.

"Swear to me that you will protect her, that you will not leave her side." Kennan looked to Aberto, grabbing his shoulder as he pleaded. "Swear it to me," he choked out.

"You need not even ask it, but I shall swear it all the same." Aberto grabbed Kennan's elbow and looked him in the eyes. "I swear I will guard and protect her all of my days, no matter how many they may be. She will never be alone from this day onward."

"See that she is not. If you don't mind, I'd like to be alone for a while." Kennan looked back out into the swamp as a tear threatened to fall down his face. I didn't understand. What had they said before I'd gotten there? What was happening?

I rushed back to where my body lay on the bed, mending my halves together. I longed to go to Kennan, but I knew that I would be found out if I did. The implications of their conversation made my stomach roil. Was Kennan leaving me? Did he have to go in order to protect me? I never should've gone. I never should've listened to a conversation that wasn't meant for my ears. Fear welled up inside of me at the possibility of living the rest of my life without him. I couldn't fathom it.

Just as I'd made my mind up to go find him, the door opened and he entered as if nothing had happened. His eyes held the same playful brightness they always did. In his hands he had a plate of food he intended to force me to eat. I looked back at his face, searching for any sign of what I'd just witnessed.

"Why are you looking at me like that?" Kennan smiled crookedly.

"Nothing, it's just," I paused trying to understand, "nothing." I shook it off. Maybe the runes were playing tricks on my mind. Cait had warned me that the darkness would do everything to pull me under. I wondered if that also meant deceiving me and making me believe horrible things.

"Are you sure? You look like you've just seen a ghost. What's going on, Izzy?" Kennan set the food on the dresser and lowered himself down to sit next to me on the bed.

"I think my mind is playing tricks on me. Maybe the exhaustion is just getting to me. I'm okay, really," I lied, wondering if I would ever be okay again.

"Promise?" Kennan asked.

"Promise, promise." As the words left my mouth, I wondered if the lie was all that white. We'd never gotten anywhere good by keeping secrets from one another, but I had no idea how I was supposed to ask him about what I'd heard. How could I? After all, I shouldn't have eavesdropped to begin with.

"Well, in that case, it is food time. No arguing." Kennan reached over to grab the plate as an idea struck me.

"What did Aberto have to say?" I waited for a reaction, something that would make me believe I'd really seen what I had but there was not so much as a shift in his demeanor as he answered.

"He wanted to talk strategy. Nothing serious. Honestly, I don't know why you couldn't have been there for the discussion. Sometimes, Aberto's reasoning makes no sense." Kennan put the plate on my lap giving me a firm look. "No more stalling, eat. I've got to go check in with Conall, but when I get back that food better be gone." He raised a brow before kissing me on the head.

"Aye, Aye!" I mock saluted.

I guess I'd imagined the whole thing. With everything we'd been through over the past year, I'd learned to read Kennan really well. Unfortunately, he showed no signs that anything was amiss at all.

Instead, he seemed completely fine. That damned darkness was going to drive me mad before I even had a chance to stop it. I should do more research on what I was up against. Maybe then I would understand what I was facing. I knew the demon's name, now I needed to know what he was capable of.

I stared at the food for a moment as if just looking at it would be enough to absorb the nutrients. Giving up, I began to shovel in the food, which happened to be some of the best gumbo I'd eaten in years. I hoovered it in, bite after bite, filling up my empty stomach until I was left with warm soup belly. I was ready to drift off to sleep and forget the day altogether. No more fights, no more drama, just the sweetness of sleep. It wasn't until it was too late that I knew I was being pulled into the dreaming. I shouted for Aberto as I faded from the mortal plane into the dreaming.

Chapter Twenty Two

I assessed the fog, hoping to spot any dangers before they could reach me. All I could hear was the sound of my own breathing and the crackling of my skin as electricity ran up and down my arms and legs. The electricity seemed to be spreading, leaving behind a burning sensation as it went. If I didn't learn to control it, I was sure it would consume me.

"Neat trick," Emmanuel said as he emerged from the fog. "Where'd you learn to do it? You aren't supposed to have that power." His scarred face curled up in distain.

"It was one of the many gifts ABERTO gave me." I shouted his name, hoping he would get the hint and show up. I wasn't ready for the last mark yet. I wasn't in any shape to fight off this asshat, either.

"Don't worry, he is already here. He won't let his precious girl come to harm. But he won't always be there to protect you. I will sneak in, I will find the chink in your armor. It is only a matter of time, and that I have in abundance." Emmanuel faded back into the fog as I fell to my knees.

"It will consume you if you let it, Izzy. You must let your anger go." Aberto towered over me as I struggled to get myself under control.

"Why is it burning? It didn't do that before?" I looked up at him as my stomach churned.

"Because it is getting stronger. This is a power not meant for any mortal to bear. I should've known that something like this may happen." Aberto swore in the old language he sometimes used. I still couldn't place what it was.

"What does that mean, Aberto? Is this going to kill me?" I looked down as the blue electricity faded into my skin.

"I do not know." He pulled me to my feet turning my arms over in his hands to check for any marks.

"He didn't get to mark me again. He knew you were here." I pulled my arms back down to my sides. "What will happen to me if this keeps getting stronger?"

"It will consume you."

"So now I have to worry about causing my own death with my lightning bolt arms and the darkness. This day just keeps getting better. If someone could just go ahead and put me out of my misery now, that would be awesome."

Aberto grabbed the back of my head forcefully, making me look in his eyes. "Do not be so fickle about your well-being. This is no joke. I will not listen as you taunt death, practically inviting it to your door step. It is time to grow up, Izzy. This is no game. This is not a joke. If you fail, then so do we all."

I pulled away from him, tears running down my face. "Don't you think I know that?" I shouted. "Every single day that I wake up with these marks is a reminder that my life is no longer my own. Every breath I take is a reminder that the darkness is coming and if I don't stop it, everything I love will disappear. I know this isn't a game. I never said it was." I sat heavily on the ground, deflated, tears coursing down my cheeks. "I'm so very tired."

"Izzy." Aberto began, but paused before he could say anything else.

"No one can help me. I'm alone in this, and that scares me more than anything," I choked out.

"You aren't alone, Izzy. Nor shall you ever be." Aberto sat on the ground next to me and grabbed my hand in his. "You will survive this."

"Do you know that, or are you just trying to reassure yourself as much as me?" I looked down to our entwined hands and felt a pang of guilt. I knew how he felt about me, but he had not pushed his feelings. I knew that any small act of encouragement I gave him was unfair so I pulled my hand away.

"A little of both, perhaps," he said, resting his hands behind him.

"Can you do the lightning thing?" I asked, anxious to change the subject. Dwelling on my demise was not going to do anyone a bit of good. It would depress me and piss Aberto off.

"I can." Aberto lifted his hand to show me a ball of blue fire burning. Only the fire was more an amorphous ball of frenetic energy. It wasn't fire at all. I looked up at his face in surprise to find that his eyes were once more glowing.

"Do my eyes do that when I get all zappy?"

"Yes. I believe that is part of the reason that the Council members banished you. You are an anomaly, something which they cannot control. Damali and Francesca have been power hungry for decades. It is a wonder they waited as long as they did to rid themselves of you. I am just sorry that it was me that ultimately became your undoing."

"Meh, you saved my butt. Even if that means I have to learn to control my temper, I'm still grateful. Maybe I could do some meditation exercises or something. Do you have any tricks?"

"Well, with you I clench my teeth and count to fifty. I found that counting to ten was not nearly long enough to keep me from wanting to throttle you."

Aberto full on smiled, almost knocking me over. That smile was dangerous.

"You are becoming quite the comedian."

"I have a great teacher. Now, you need to rest. I will stay in the dreaming and keep guard, but I am blocking you." Aberto lifted his hands to my face, gently holding me as if I would break at a moment's notice.

"Okay. See you tomorrow?" Tears still threatened to flow, but I knew that Aberto was ultimately right, just as he always was. Not that I would be admitting to that any time soon.

"We have much to accomplish." Just like that the calming blanket of nothing sank in.

Arguing pulled me from my deep sleep. I opened my eyes to see light creeping through the curtains and realized I'd slept straight through the morning. It was almost noon. I sat up trying to find the source of the argument only to find Conall and Sena having a heated discussion, in my room, with no one else in sight.

"Umm, hi?" I muttered groggily.

"See, I told you she was fine. There is no reason in the world to go waking up an exhausted, marked up, prophesized one when you don't need to. She woke up just fine on her own." Sena stomped her foot petulantly causing Conall to roll his one good eye.

"Well, you guys arguing sort of woke me up." I yawned loudly trying to rub the sleep from my eyes.

"Oh, sorry," Sena mumbled quickly as she headed toward the bed to sit on the edge. "Since you are up, perhaps you can tell Do..., I mean Conall, that he is out of his mind if he thinks I'm going back to the Council with him. This is my home, these are my people."

"Sorry to tell you, but none of us are welcome there, Conall. Didn't Kennan tell you?"

"Tell me what?" Conall stood, rooted in place. A look of trepidation replaced his indignation.

"Umm, we were banished?" I half asked.

"What did you do, Izzy?" Conall looked at me like I'd intentionally gone in there and caused a ruckus.

"I just showed up. Blame those crazy old bats that deposed me," I said, doing my best not to get angry. Sena was sitting awfully close to me, and I didn't want to zap her into a smoldering pile of ash. Conall would be even madder if I did that.

"What was said, exactly?" Conall still had the "this is totally your fault, Izzy" tone. It was really irritating how he always blamed me for the mess. Even if it was normally my fault.

"There was mention of me being an abomination, which caused me to zap the desk into a pile of ash. Oh, and then they pretty much told me what I told Elaine. The whole, none shall give you shelter and any found harboring you will be banished. So, since you were on team Izzy, you got banished by association. Didn't you wonder why Eleanor was here?"

"She is a lot like my mother, she often shows up in surprising places." Conall moved further towards the bed but paused as a thought crossed his mind. "Do you mean to tell me that Ian stood with them against you?"

"Yeah, right. No, he and Molly are in Chicago."

"Why is he not here?" Conall seemed angry that Ian wouldn't come to our aid.

"Because he doesn't have to be, and I won't force him to return to the Order until it is on his own terms. There are some things that can't be rushed, Conall."

"But we need his help to protect you!" Conall practically screamed as if I were being completely dense.

Sena rose from the bed and moved towards him slowly as if he were a caged animal. I could suddenly see the wolf in him, chomping at the surface. When she got close enough, she placed a hand on his shoulder and whispered something lyrical that managed to draw his anger back. The animal disappeared and he breathed heavily.

"Sorry, Izzy," he muttered before giving Sena a wary look and disappearing.

"Should've known I would end up with the wolfman," Sena said thoughtfully as she returned to sitting on my bed.

"Why in the world would you say that?" I scooted over to give her more room as she flopped back against the pillows next to me.

"My name, and my talent." She shrugged as if it were nothing exceptionally strange.

"What does your name mean, exactly? And what sort of talent do you have, what did you just do to Conall?"

"My name means 'the moon'." She paused as I burst into laughter. "Yeah, yuck it up, Izzy. At least I have a full name."

"Hey, my name means something, too. So don't get all high and mighty over there or I will zap you into a pile of ash and let wolfman pee on it when he wolfs out."

"That is just plain mean." Sena glared at me. "Well, Miss Prophecy, what does your name mean?"

"Eleanor looked it up. She thought I should know that my destiny had been written from birth. Ultimately, it just made me want to smack her. My name means 'God is My Oath'." Sena stared at me, wide eyed. "Yeah, I know. Talk about being predestined for something. At least you aren't alone, right?"

"True. As for the other question you asked, my talent is calming. Mona says I am like the moon itself, helping to control the ebb and flow of people's emotions."

"Can you just stay close to me until I get this X-men power crap under control?"

"Promise not to turn me into a pile of ash and let Conall pee on me?" She looked at me wary for a moment.

"Promise," I smiled. "Now, I really need to get up and get dressed. Oh, and pee. I REALLY need to do that," I said standing up. It hadn't hit me until then.

"Well, do you need help getting dressed again?"

"No, I think I can handle it this morning. Just stay close today, if you don't mind."

"I honestly have nothing better to do, and it beats facing Conall and his relentless questioning." Sena made no motion to get up from the bed.

"Okay, well I will meet you in the hall then, if you don't mind." I tried to give her a pointed look, but it was probably coming off a bit wonky what with the desperate need to use the bathroom.

"Don't fall in," she said, getting up and leaving the room.

I slowly made my way over to my bag, pulling out a pair of stretchy yoga pants and a slouchy sweatshirt. I hoped that I could fight the darkness in comfy clothes, otherwise I was hosed. The thought reminded me of Cait, as she approached the demon in her flowing white dress. There was something beautiful about it that made me rethink the whole dying in yoga pants thing. Nah, yoga pants were way more comfortable. I wasn't going out in style, but at least I would be cozy. By the time I left the room, after cleaning myself up in the bathroom, there was a small group waiting for me.

"We have much to discuss," Aberto said, holding his arm out for me to walk in front of him.

"What's going on?" I asked Kennan, who had been talking to Sena as I left the room.

"Eleanor and Mona have something they wish to discuss with you. It pertains to you being so tired. They think it may help." Kennan seemed hesitant, as if whatever they had planned wasn't going to be all that pleasant.

"Will it hurt?"

"No more than your other markings," Aberto supplied.

"A simple yes would have sufficed," I quipped.

"I thought that the rest would put you in a more pleasant mood," Aberto said solemnly. The man had no appreciation for sarcasm.

"Well, where are we going? And does everyone really need to be there?" I looked behind at the trail of people. Not only were Conall, Sena, Aberto, and Kennan with me, but there were a whole host of other Guardians. Some I recognized from the Division and some were obviously part of the Order.

"We feel it is best to be with you at all times from here on out, in case the bridge is completed," Conall answered.

"Right, well this will be a ton of fun." I turned my attention back to where I was going. I was just letting Kennan lead me, with no idea of where he would take me. Trust was a glorious thing sometimes.

"Wait here. I need to see if they are ready." Kennan moved into a hazy room, leaving me standing awkwardly in the hall with everyone staring at me.

"What?" I finally blurted.

"Is it true that you carry an electric charge within you now?" one of the Guardians asked.

"Yes," I muttered before turning my back on them to face the door. I was getting tired of being looked at like some sort of oddity. I was absolutely not an abomination. Nope, no siree, I was completely normal. No need for the stares. If they kept it up, I may just run away and join the circus. At least there I would get paid for people staring at me. Oh, maybe I could start charging admission to the Izzy show. Just as I started to formulate my amazing costume and backdrop, Kennan came back out into the hall.

"They are ready. Just Izzy and Aberto." Kennan motioned us in.

"Um, Sena should come, too," I said nervously. Now that I knew she could keep my crazy in check, I was going to cart her around like a security blanket.

"You can't scream or react in there, do you understand?" Kennan leveled her with a stony gaze.

"Okay," Sena said, wide-eyed.

"Let's go, then. The rest of you wait out here, please?" Kennan pinned Conall with his eyes. He knew that if he were in his place, he'd be trying to charge in with his Seer.

"Alright," Conall said, turning his back to the door to guard it.

Chapter Twenty Three

A hazy room filled with fragrant smoke enveloped me as I walked into the darkness. I struggled to gain my bearings in the dim light. The vision of my aunt and Eleanor sent chills down my spine. They were both seated perfectly still, with their eyes closed muttering something over smoking coals. I was starting to get nervous about whatever this was. Whenever there was chanting and smoke, it couldn't be a good thing. It reminded me of some voodoo witch-doctor stuff. Well, at least the stuff I'd seen in movies.

"What do you people plan to do to me?" I wasn't jumping in blindly. No Siree Bob, not this time.

"They are going to blunt the impact of the runes. This is our Hail Mary, a last resort," Kennan whispered, but my confusion was obvious, making him continue, "It should provide more clarity so that the darkness doesn't seem quite so appealing."

"Pray tell how do they hope to do this?" I looked down at the glowing coals and had a sinking suspicion of what was about to come. My fear took over and a blue spark shot up my arm. Sena moved toward me quickly, whispering something in my ear. My fear disappeared as if on the wind. I was left feeling amazingly calm. "Thanks."

"Just don't zap me, and we're good," Sena promised.

"I can handle that." I paused. "Probably."

"Izzy, this is a last resort. Our last chance to intercede on your behalf. This will not cut the tie, only dull its effects on you. If you wish to continue on as you are, you may." Eleanor had opened her eyes, only to pin me in place with her stare.

"You know I'm going to do go through with whatever this is." I paused looking at the coals hesitantly. "I just wasn't exactly mentally prepared for the whole being grilled like a brisket thing. A little heads up next time would be super awesome."

"Do not be melodramatic, young lady. We intend to do no such thing." And there it was, my mom's 'You're in trouble' voice right out of my aunt.

"Fine," I huffed, sitting heavily on a floor pillow. "What do I need to do?"

"You will need to change into this." Aberto handed me a dress that eerily resembled the one Cait had died in. I tried to tamp down my panic but it got the best of me. Sena yelled something from across the room that managed to bring my angst into check.

"Do you come in pill form?" I asked Sena, only half joking.

"You wish. You wouldn't need me around if that were the case," Sena said, causing me to wonder what her story was. She seemed terrified that I would fade away at a moments' notice. I just hoped that I would be around long enough to show her she was wrong.

"Yes, I would," I promised before heading to the corner and donning the dress behind a screen. I tried my best to shake of the image of Cait and face whatever torture the old hags, I mean Eleanor and my aunt, had in store.

"Are you ready to get started?" I nodded at my aunt who motioned for me to lay on the cushions stretched across the floor. "You can't go on a walkabout. You have to stay and the let the binding stitch together on both planes."

"I know the drill," I sighed, trying to find my center. All I needed was to fricassee the people I cared about as they tried to fix me. I sucked in a deep breath as I felt the heat of the first coal approach.

"Son of a donkey butted, biscuit eating, bastard!" I cursed as the pain radiated from the rune. It was as if the rune was protecting itself against the binding. It hurt worse than anything I'd ever experienced. "I can't do it. I can't," I sobbed trying to yank my arm away from the oncoming coal.

"Hold her down!" My aunt shouted. "You must do this, Izzy. Otherwise you won't have the strength to defend yourself. So suck it up, buttercup. This is happening."

I felt strong arms press me back down into the cushions. My shoulders were braced so that I couldn't move and inch. I looked up expecting to see Kennan, instead it was Aberto holding me down. I looked across the room to find Kennan slowly backing out of the room, his jaw clenched and his face green.

"He can't bear to see you suffer. It is better that he is not here," Aberto whispered. "Now focus on something. Center yourself."

I looked up into his unfathomably blue eyes and let myself get lost in them. I felt the part of his soul that resided in me leap at the recognition. The smoldering coal came into contact with the first rune, causing me to arch up and close my eyes. The pain was unbearable. How was I supposed to get through more of this?

"Izzy." Aberto's voice sounded so far away. "Izzy, open your eyes and look at me."

I opened my eyes as tears leaked through the corners of my eyes. "I can't do it." I sobbed.

"You must," Aberto said calmly. "Would you like to hear a story?"

"Now? You want to tell me a story now?" I was incredulous. Of all the times for Aberto to be in a sharing mood, this seemed the least convenient.

"I do." He smiled softly. "Keep your eyes trained on me as I tell my tale. If you close your eyes, I stop talking. Do we have a deal?"

"Okay. You have a deal." I stared up into his eyes, his hair cascaded around his face, forming a curtain between us and the outside world.

"This is the story of when I saw you again for the first time after many years."

"But you said you had always been there," I interrupted causing Aberto to arch a brow.

"No interruptions. I was always in the dreaming, waiting for the day you found your way back. Remember when I told you that I took away your memories of me and the dreaming? Well, as they faded, you did as well. You quit coming to the dreaming and you forgot about me altogether. Then, one day, you showed back up. It was right after your Grandmother died. You came into the dreaming, weeping and lost." Aberto paused looking down into my face as another coal came to rest on a rune.

"Story, more story," I pleaded, anxious to think of anything but the pain radiating through my extremities.

"I came to you that day, only I wasn't sure it was you. The last time I'd seen you, you were a child. What I found was a woman. I was surprised at the time that had passed, unaware that so many years had slipped through my fingers. You came stumbling into the dreaming, the same blinding beacon you'd been on the day you were born. I knew, the moment I saw the light appear that you'd come back. Your time was drawing near." Aberto looked sadly into my eyes. "But that was the day that I knew it was you. I've known you my whole life, Izzy. From my first breath, I saw you coming. I didn't know who you were, I didn't know when you were; I just knew that you *were*. After thousands of years, I'd forgotten. The memory of you had been covered by countless years and countless struggles. But the moment I saw you, with your tear stained face standing in the dreaming, it all came back."

"What did you remember?" I winced as they pulled the coal away from my arm. I knew I had more to go, and I needed the distraction.

"I remembered the vision I'd been born with. The vision of a Seer that was loved by many. She was a bright light in a time of darkness. She caused men to rise up in her wake, to fight for her, to battle the darkness and bring the light. She was, is, loved beyond compare."

"Well, that wasn't true at all. I just got ejected from the Council," I half yelped as another coal made its way toward my leg and the rune tried to fight back. I tried to look toward my aunt, whose face was covered in sweat as she pressed hard on the coal, fighting against the rune's power.

"Izzy, look at me. Focus on me." I turned back to Aberto, trying to erase the image of my glowing flesh.

"What, what did you remember?" I barely muttered.

"I remembered that I loved you. From my first breath."

"Aberto." I began only to have him shake his head.

"No, you mistake my meaning. I do not mean love in that way, although over the time I have known you that love has emerged. You know I will never press my feelings upon you. I know where your heart lies, and I will honor that until my dying breath. The love I speak of is of a different sort. Wherever you are, whatever nonsense you get yourself into, I knew the day I took my first breath that I would always be there. I would protect you, I would guard you, and I would keep you from harm. You have taught me what it is to be selfless." Aberto's eyes misted over as he continued. "Seeing you again reminded me of the selfish man I'd become. I knew that you needed me to be more than I'd become. Kennan and Conall are right to be angry with me. I should have interceded years ago with Cait. I was lost then. I was consumed by my hate and disgust with what the world had become. I didn't see any light left in it, and then you came back. You reminded me that even in the darkness, there is still light. You saved me, Izzy."

Those were the last words I heard before I lost the battle and succumbed to unconsciousness. The pain had become too unbearable, my mind gave in. Aberto's words echoed through my mind as I drifted.

Chapter Twenty Four

Floating in the oblivion of the pain induced insta-coma, I began to remember Aberto more clearly. I'd been getting snippets of memories from my childhood, but I couldn't quite remember who he was to me, or why I'd trusted him so implicitly. Then I saw it, the moment he'd just told me about. I watched as he approached me. I must have been about twenty-three, right after my Grams died.

I stood eyeing the fog warily as my mother yelled at me. Aberto approached me slowly, as if he were a wild animal testing the water for crocodiles. As he came closer, I tilted my head in recognition. Something in me remembered. He lifted his hand to my face slowly and began to speak.

"Hello again." He smiled, sadly.

"Again?" I stood stock still, afraid to move a muscle.

"Sadly, and sadly the next time we meet you will not remember me either. You aren't ready to be here yet, Izzy. Your time will come. Go now, live your life, for much will change soon."

"What will change? Who are you?"

"Everything has its season," Aberto promised in his traditionally cryptic way.

And just like that, the memory swept away. I could see the exact moment he'd changed my memory. I began flipping back through my own memories, sifting them until I found every single one. At every stage of my life he had been there, watching over me. How was I ever going to repay him? More importantly, how could he have kept quiet about it all of this time while I was being such a snot to him?

As I lay, drifting in my subconscious, I wondered how I even felt about all of it. I knew that a part of me called out for Aberto. I could no longer deny that. But my heart belonged to Kennan in a way that it could never belong to anyone else. Kennan was my happily ever after. No matter what wayward feelings might have cropped up for Aberto, my heart was sure where it belonged. I still wasn't even sure if the way I felt for Aberto was because of his soul residing inside of my own, or if it was some sort of affection held over from my childhood, or something else entirely. What I did know, was it wouldn't change anything. No matter its source.

Grasping at reality, I pulled myself back to consciousness. I awoke with my skin feeling as though it were on fire. Panic began to build inside of me, until I heard Aberto's voice again.

"You are almost done. Stay with me," he whispered.

"Okay," I breathed, as the tears began tracing pathways down my face once more.

"Just one more and we will be finished, Izzy," my aunt's reassuring voice promised.

As the coal made its way toward the last rune, my body felt as though it were ready to jump from the table and walk itself away. Whatever these runes were, their protections were fierce. The only thought tracing through my mind was that this whole mess better be worth it. If I came out of this room still feeling drawn and exhausted, but with new and improved scars, I would be furious.

"AAAHHHHH!" I screamed out, arching my back as they cauterized the last of the runes on my thigh.

"All done, Izzy." Eleanor patted my arm gently.

"Kennan," I wheezed.

"I will get your Guardian." Aberto stood to walk away, but I grabbed his hand to hold him in place.

"Thank you, for today, and for every other day that you have been there." Tears welled in my eyes from the pain.

"It has been my pleasure." Aberto slowly released my hand and headed out to get Kennan.

"Well, you didn't get all sparky. I think you should consider this a success," Sena beamed.

"Yay!" I choked out.

"Izzy?" Kennan asked as he entered the room. The strain on his face broke me. I knew that he hated anything that caused me pain, but he knew that we had to try whatever we could to stop the coming darkness.

"I'm okay. I need some help back up to the room though. I feel like I need to lie still for a bit." I didn't even get a chance to finish before he carefully scooped me up in his arms, avoiding all of my runes. "Oh, but Eleanor, I have some questions!" I shouted as we left the room.

"I'll come with you, then. You need to rest, so it is probably best that we just discuss whatever this is where you will be comfortable."

Kennan carried me into our room, gently placing me on the bed. We were followed in by a whole herd of Guardians, much to my chagrin.

"Can't they wait outside? I promise to announce the demon's arrival when it happens." I looked to Kennan wide-eyed. There was no way I could get through the next few days with twenty Guardians following me everywhere. I would go insane before the demon could even show up.

"Gentlemen, she would like some privacy," Kennan snickered.

"How would you like it if you had to have everyone following you around?" I grumbled to an amused Kennan.

"Well cared for?" Kennan ventured.

I responded with a glare, effectively shutting him up. I wondered if I was getting better at my mean face. Or maybe my eyes were glowing again. Glowing eyes seemed to shut everyone up.

"What did you wish to discuss, Izzy?" Eleanor asked, wiping the sweat from her brow. She looked like she'd just run a marathon through the depths of hell.

"The demon, Sonneillon. I know that you have been doing some research, and I want to know everything I can about him. If I learned anything from 80's cartoons, it's 'Knowledge is Power'."

"Well, not much is known of him. He is the demon of hatred and is fourth in line for the throne of hell," Eleanor supplied.

"Yeah, but what is his deal. All demons have something they do to twist the world, what does he do?" I longed to understand what I was up against. I just hoped that Eleanor would have more information than what I already knew.

"He turns men against one another, whispers in their ears things that will incite violence. Friend will turn against friend, brother against brother, until the world is covered in blood. His thirst for hate is unquenchable." Eleanor's fear shone brightly in her eyes.

"But why this demon? I don't understand why they didn't choose another one to come and wreak havoc. There must be something about this one that makes it more appealing." I settled back against the pillows, mulling over the possible implications of the choice.

"If what you've said is true, then the Old One that seeks to bring justice to the world intends to turn those he feels undeserving against one another. Sonneillon only has power over the weak. Those that have broken spirits to begin with will fall prey to him more easily. If it is a cleansing they seek, then this is the demon that will provide."

"What is the demon's weakness?" Surely he had to have one. Everything had a weakness.

"In Catholicism, he is believed to be the adversary of St. Stephen. St. Stephen is considered the first Christian martyr." Eleanor seemed to be regaining her composure as she slipped into what I'd dubbed her professorial role.

"So, in a nut shell, dying for something bigger than myself is the demon's weakness. Which is why Cait's sacrifice was its undoing. So this really is my only option, isn't it?" I looked up into Eleanor's face, reality finally crashing in on me. I couldn't breathe.

"Izzy, there has to be some other way," Kennan promised, rushing to my side.

"But there isn't. I see that now more clearly than I ever have before. This is the prophecy. This is my destiny. No matter how much we might want to change it, we can't." My resolve was hardening. I knew that I would do what it took, no matter the cost.

"But we must," Kennan pleaded.

"Eleanor, I need to talk to Kennan alone." I never took my eyes off of him, I knew that I needed him, and in that moment, he was the most important thing in the world to me.

"Of course, Izzy." Eleanor got up and exited the room quietly as Kennan and I stayed locked in one another's eyes.

"We can't let them win." Kennan's eyes misted over.

"If I don't do this, we will be letting them win. Kennan, the gods, God, whoever the heck is running this madhouse, have spoken. I've been told countless times that the answer lies within me, that I must be willing to give of myself to end this. I'm running on borrowed time as it is, my love. I should've died months ago, when I freed the Seers. This time is not my own, and now I must pay the price for the time I have taken."

"I can't, Izzy. I can't just let you go. I have to fight, I have to do something."

"Then fight, help me hold the demon back long enough to do what must be done." I pulled him down next to me on the bed, longing to be close to him. "Just promise me something."

"I don't know that I can, Izzy." Kennan's voice broke, almost undoing me.

"I haven't even asked you yet," I whispered softly, hoping that I could convince him to listen.

"But I know what you are going to ask me. You're going to ask me to promise that your death will not be my undoing. You want me to promise that I will go on living after you've gone. You want me to promise to protect the people you love. I can't, Izzy. You've been my world for longer than I can remember. When you leave, so does my purpose." Kennan looked into my eyes, a tear threatening to leak from his eye. I struggled to hold myself together.

"Well, I was just going to ask you to promise to give that demon hell in your Hulk-ish state." I smiled warmly at him. "But, the other stuff is important, too. And you can go on living, because Ian and Conall will need you. After all, you've been bounced from the Council thanks to me. At least promise me that you will try."

"I promise that I will try," Kennan breathed out, his promise settling over me.

"And promise not to try and stop me from doing what must be done."

"I promise that I will try," Kennan said stiffly. "But, Izzy, a world without you in it is not a world in which I want to live."

"Likewise, Kennan. But neither is a world in which everyone I love suffers because I was too selfish to act. I would never be able to face myself in the mirror again. It's time we stopped running from the truth and face it head on. Are you with me?"

"Always, Izzy. Always," Kennan promised, and I knew it was the truth. He always would be with me, no matter the days, no matter what may lie ahead.

"Then just stay with me, here, now. Let's just take this time out for us," I begged, hoping that for one night I could forget it all and live in the moment. The future couldn't steal this from me. No matter what the Fates had in store, I could have this.

"Deal." Kennan raised his hand to stroke my face gently, staring down into my eyes pleadingly. So many unsaid words left hidden behind the sadness.

The hours slipped slowly by as we lay there, entwined in one another's arms. We laughed about our predestined meeting and our life in Chicago before everything fell apart. We lay silently, just listening to one another breathe. The moments ticked by, and as time slipped away, I understood that this was our goodbye. But what a beautiful goodbye it had been. I counted myself lucky that I knew enough about my future that I could tell the person I loved most in the world exactly what he meant to me before I was gone. I silently lifted up a prayer that he would keep on living after I'd gone. A world without Kennan O'Malley would be a dreary place indeed.

Chapter Twenty Five

All too soon, night called out, reminding me that I needed to rest. I could feel the coming storm, raging in the distance. Static charged the air as the darkness loomed, I knew it was time. Everything was going to end soon. As a yawn escaped my mouth, Kennan pulled me closer to his body. It was practically an acrobatic feat to not brush against any of runes, but tonight, it seemed it no longer mattered.

"Do you want me to block you?" Kennan ran is fingers through my hair, causing me to drift further towards sleep.

"No, it is best that this ends as soon as it can. If that means that I must be marked tonight, then so be it."

"We could have one more day," Kennan pleaded.

"One more day would never be enough. I would always want for more. It is best to stop running and face what is coming head-on," I whispered silently, hoping that he understood. An eternity with him would never be long enough. One more day would be nothing more than a tease.

"I know you're right, but that doesn't mean I have to like it." Kennan pulled me close, kissing me deeply. "I love you Mrs. O'Malley, forever and for always."

"I love you Mr. Boone, forever and for always." I smiled up at him brightly, wondering how long it would take him to respond.

"I would take your name any day." He kissed me once more, softly, before whispering "Sweet dreams."

"Goodnight," I muttered as the last of my awareness slipped away.

It was the same vision or dream I'd been having for months. I stood on the clouds watching the Angels rage a war, only this time things were different. Events moved before my eyes as if they were moving through some viscous fluid. Nothing happened in real time, and as I made my way through the battlefield, I could see the strain on each of the faces as they battled in the war that would not end.

"It's a pity, is it not?" A man's voice startled me from my examination.

"Well, you're new." I turned, wide-eyed to face the man that the voice belonged to. Only, he wasn't exactly a man, what with the giant wings rising up from his back and the blinding glow radiating from his body. He wasn't a man at all.

"I am Uriel." He bowed deeply, his downy wings dusting the ground as he went.

"Okay. I'm guessing I should know who you are. They didn't give me the handbook, so really, I've got no clue." I stared in amazement at him, totally forgetting the battle around me. I was sure there was some sort of protocol that I should've been following. I mean, there had to be some sort of precedence for meeting with angels. Should I bow? Swear my allegiance? Offer up a goat?

"I am the source, the Origin of the Seers and Guardians. Some have called me the 'Fire of God'," Uriel supplied, tilting his head to the side in question as if he were listening in on my internal dialogue. I'm sure he probably was.

"So, whatcha doing in my dream?" I asked slowly. Plowing right on through seemed to be the way to go these days. I just hoped it would work with this guy. Even more, I hoped that he would not prove to be as evasive as all of his creations.

"I've come to tell you, your day draws nigh," Uriel provided. Thanks, Captain Obvious.

"Well, I sort of knew that already. Anything else? Any messages you want me to pass on to the Old Ones. Oh, by the way, that Emmanuel guy you created has gone totally batshit crazy. Just, you know, in case you weren't aware. Did you create them, because I sort of thought the whole Creation thing was God's department." I couldn't shut myself up. I was standing there, talking to what I could only imagine was an archangel and all I could do was yammer. My brain had finally snapped. I'd known that it was only a matter of time, I just hoped that it would've waited until after the defeating the darkness bit.

"No, I am not the creator, I am the source. The overseer perhaps would be a better term. And yes, I am aware of Emmanuel, but like all mankind, Seers and Guardians are given a choice. Even the ones of old. He will serve his purpose, as do all men." Uriel looked slightly bored with my questions which was causing me to get really indignant.

"So, we really are all just a bunch of game pieces to you lot, aren't we?" Now, I was just getting angry.

"This is no game. This is a war. A war of darkness pressing against light since the dawn of time. There will always be upswings and downswings, but we must keep fighting. We must use all that is at our hands to ensure that man survives." His eyes lit up with a churning fire as he seemed to grow ever taller.

"Okay, so what is all this then? Why do I keep seeing this?" I gestured around me at the angels and demons battling.

"This is a reminder. You are not the only ones that must fight. The fight exists on all planes, Izzy. Even on ours. Yours is not the only sacrifice, nor shall it be the last," Uriel provided.

"Cait," I whispered.

"Yes. She did something that was never asked of her. The demon never would have been strong enough to remain on the corporeal plane for long, yet she still sacrificed herself to ensure the world's safety."

"But did you ask this of me? How can I feel like it is even a choice, when my fate was written before I took my first breath?" I'd been struggling with the knowledge that I was powerless to control my own destiny. Maybe I could finally find some concrete answers.

"Because you do have a choice. You can walk away, and leave man to deal with the repercussions." Awesome, more "it is your choice" propaganda.

"No, I can't," I stated the obvious. I would be a monster if I walked away and left the world to burn. The vision of Chicago raced through my mind anew, the darkness consuming the man, eating away at him like some sort of virus.

"Which is precisely why you were chosen to fulfill this calling. Go forth bravely, Izzy. The fight has just begun." Uriel motioned towards the ground.

The battle sped up around me as Uriel faded away. The shrieks of the demons echoed around the clouds, sending chills down my spine. I moved forward, to the place I knew I must go. To my end.

I fell through the clouds, down to where the battle raged. I looked at the people I loved. The time was here. I embraced the demon, hoping that it would end how it did every other time I'd had the vision.

"Oh, that's precious. You're giving him a hug? I'm sure that will make everything better for him. Solve all of those pesky hate problems he seems to have. Are you going to hug me as well? Maybe I wasn't hugged enough early in life. Perhaps that is why I'm doing this now." Emmanuel's glee made me want to throat punch the bastard.

"Well, get it over with. I know why you're here. Just slap the last mark on and let's get this little game of chicken over with."

"You do realize you will never win? There is no scenario in which you come out of this unscathed," Emmanuel mocked.

"I'm fully aware of what I'm about to face." Not a bit of inflection graced my words. I was wrung out, tired from the game. I just wanted it to be done.

"You know you won't be able to just hug it out with the demon, correct?" Emmanuel seemed to be enjoying himself, mocking me at every turn. I would really love it if I could somehow kill the meddling moron while taking down the demon. If was I truly lucky, they may just be connected.

"If you could shut the hell up and mark me, I would really appreciate it." I stood, rooted in place, unwilling to show any signs of weakness. It was time.

"It would be my pleasure." His voice hissed the last word as the final rune appeared on my chest. "Time's up, princess. See you soon."

"I'm so kicking that demon's ass," I muttered as I sought to leave the dreaming. "And then I'm coming for you!"

Chapter Twenty Six

I opened my eyes to a bright world. The running was over, the fight had finally reached my door. Inhaling slowly, I tried to focus not on what was just around the corner, but what was here and now. I looked over to find Kennan staring at me, a thousand feelings passed between us, but none were said. I couldn't do what needed to be done if I kept saying goodbye. Time was up, and we needed to formulate a plan.

"It's done," I whispered.

"I know." Kennan's strained reply threatened to tear me apart.

"We need to make a plan. Find somewhere that we can fight. I don't know how much time it will take for Sonneillon to get here. For all I know, he could show up at any moment." I moved toward my bag, trying to keep myself in motion. If I stopped, I would never be able to face it. Just looking at Kennan was painful. How could I ever leave him?

"Let's get dressed and find Eleanor and Mona. Perhaps they will have a better idea of what we should expect." Kennan's subdued tone told me that I wasn't alone. His feelings mirrored my own.

"What about last time? How long was it after Cait's last mark appeared that the demon came crashing onto this plane?"

"We had a day. Just a day." Kennan rubbed his hand down his face. We were both reluctant to leave the room, knowing that it was probably the last time we would have alone together.

"Then we don't have any time to waste. We have to get moving," I choked out. Tears threatened to drown me as I dug through my bag, trying to find something to wear.

"I know." Kennan pulled me close, kissing the top of my head as he did. "But before we do, I need you to know that no matter what happens, no matter the outcome of the next few days, I love you. Just try to remember that."

"I've never doubted it." I breathed him in, relishing in the comfort of his scent. It would all be over soon. I just hoped that someday we would be together again. Surely God wasn't so cruel as to keep us apart for the rest of time.

"Time's up," he muttered, moving away from me to get up and put some clothes on.

I felt my throat tighten as tears threatened to fall. It was all too much. I couldn't understand what kind of cruel world would give me such happiness only to snatch it away. I suppose it wouldn't really be a sacrifice if I didn't have so much to lose. No matter how I looked at it, this whole situation sucked.

"Can you ask Eleanor and Mona to meet us downstairs?" I asked. [N1] Kennan had managed to get dressed already and I needed some time away from him if I had any hope of keeping myself together.

"I can." Kennan moved to the door, looking back at me for a moment. The look in his eyes ripped my heart out. There was nothing I could do to ease the pain.

I smiled warmly as he left the room. I had to be strong. I couldn't falter now, when my actions mattered the most. It was time I faced the music, got everyone ready, and ended this darkness. I slowly combed through my meager clothing choices and picked out the most comfortable thing I could find. Screw going out in style, I was exhausted and I would be doing good to even put the durn clothes on.

I pulled my pants up slowly over the cauterized runes, careful to avoid the sensitive skin. I did have to give it to them though, whatever they had done had given me more energy. I didn't feel like a big wind could blow me over any longer. When I came to my shirt, I paused to look at the ugly mark in the mirror. It covered my entire chest, a large glowing symbol of my imminent destruction. I could feel the pull of the darkness, the temptation to submit as I looked into the mirror.

"I will not falter." I told my reflection, causing my eyes to spark blue. I looked more closely and found that the hazel of my eyes was almost completely faded. In its place was the glowing blue I'd seen in Aberto's eyes and, come to think of it, Uriel's eyes. I wondered when the glowing eyes had faded from our DNA. What an odd thought to have at a time like this. I shook myself from my ridiculous thoughts and sought to refocus my attention on what was really important.

I pulled on my shirt and headed out into the hall, carefully ignoring every one of the Guardians waiting there. I walked with purpose down the stairs. I needed goals, I needed something to focus on. If I didn't keep moving forward, I would never move at all. I would stay rooted in place, perpetually frozen in this moment with Kennan. But we weren't made to stay still, nor were we made to move backward. The only way for me to go was toward my destiny.

"Izzy?" Aberto's voice pulled me from my thoughts.

"Yeah?" I looked up at him, an empty shell of myself.

"What has transpired?" Concern etched his features as he pulled me to a stop.

"What's happened? You should say that instead." I paused for a second before moving on, no stopping for me.

"What's happened? Izzy, stop and look at me. Tell me what you know," Aberto pleaded.

"It's time. I know that Uriel is the one that has been talking to me. I know that the heavens knew of Emmanuel's plans for as long as he has been in existence. I know that I only have one day left on this earth. I know that this predestination stuff sucks. Mostly, I know that I've been living on borrowed time, and it is time to repay that debt." I rushed through everything, hoping that if I just kept going, I would find a way to make it.

"You owe nothing." Aberto's eyes flamed.

"I owe everything." I reached up and touched his face the way he had mine a thousand time throughout my life. "Please don't make this any harder on me than it already is."

"What would you have me do?" His voice came out strained.

"Help me. Help Kennan and Conall, even Ian when I'm gone. Help them to keep fighting."

"Izzy, there is something I feel I should tell you." Aberto looked pained, as if the words were stuck.

"Nothing you can say will make this any different. This is the end, and I've accepted that. There is no sense in dwelling on it. So promise me, promise you will help them."

"I will do your bidding until the end of my days, Izzy." Aberto pulled me closely against his skin. It was the first time he'd embraced me when I wasn't in the process of trying to die. It was strangely comforting.

"We need to get moving. We don't have much more time." I pulled away from him and moved the rest of the way towards the sitting room where everyone was waiting.

I walked in and everyone's eyes shifted toward me. I knew it was time to put on my leader pants and be strong. If I failed now, everyone in this room would eventually fall. Personally, I felt that one person's fall was more than enough.

"We need to find a place to make a stand. Somewhere in the open that will be easy to defend. I will need help getting close to the demon, which means that any of you Guardians with extra talents will have to transform, morph, suit-up, whatever you call it. In my vision, it always happens somewhere near an abandoned church. It is crumbling in the background and the gravestones are worn from years of exposure. Do any of you know where this might be?"

"The church, on the edge of the swamp. No one has been there in years. It's super creepy," Sena supplied. Everyone turned toward her at her last remark. "What? It is," she huffed.

"Okay, well that is where we need to be. So, what can we do to make that happen? Do y'all have a pontoon boat hanging around somewhere? Is there a trail we can take? How long will it take to get there?" I needed to keep moving, it was working. No stopping now.

"Slow down, Izzy. We will figure this all out. First, we must prepare the Guardians." My aunt reached for my hand.

"I don't have time to slow down and neither do any of you. It is coming, I can feel it move closer with every breath I take. If we do nothing, if we do not act soon, all of this struggle will be for nothing. Don't make everything I've gone through over the past few years be for nothing. Y'all have an hour to get marked and then we are moving. I'm tired of waiting for my destiny to catch up with me. I would rather go out and face it head on."

"I will do the markings," Aberto said, slipping out of existence only to pop back in moments later with his tattooing implements.

"Izzy, can I talk to you for a moment?" Kennan pulled me to the side of the room, away from everyone's prying eyes.

"What is it?" I asked, afraid to truly look him in the eyes.

"When this change comes, I won't be myself. I don't remember who I truly am. The rage takes over, and all I can see is destruction. I don't want your last memories of me to be that." Kennan looked pained. I knew how much he hated turning into the beasty, but I also knew that we needed him.

"We need you, Kennan. I know who you are. I know what you really are. In all of your many forms, I know that you love me. I know that you will do what needs to be done to help stop this. So, please, for me, do this," I begged.

"Just remember, this is not who I truly am."

"I know, Kennan. Just like Conall isn't really a wolf." I looked up into his eyes, trying to convey that I understood.

"Well, he is kind of like a wild animal." Kennan smiled in Conall's direction. Aberto was working on his mark as we watched.

"It's time, Kennan. We can't keep delaying. I'm ready. You have to let me go," I whispered so that only Kennan could hear.

"I will never be able to let you go, but I will let you do what you feel you must. I'm not going to hold you back, not anymore," Kennan promised, pulling me close.

"I love you, big guy." I breathed in the smell of him, letting it soothe my anxious soul.

"Love you more, Red," he muttered, hugging me tightly. He placed a gentle kiss on the top of my head, bringing back a thousand memories in the process.

I pulled away, turning my back toward Kennan as I moved out of the room. Staying there would weaken my resolve. They didn't need me for the markings, so I sought the comfort of the swamp. I walked towards the doors, thinking back on the past few years and wondering at how much my life had changed. The dense swamp air greeted me like a wet blanket as I moved outside. I walked to the edge of the water and stared down, wondering at how easy it would be to end everything now. I wouldn't have to suffer any longer.

"Do not let the darkness win." My aunt's voice drew me from my thoughts. "You are too strong to let that happen."

"I'm not strong at all," I replied honestly.

"You were chosen for a reason." I turned toward my aunt, and I realized she was channeling someone else.

"Uriel?"

"You are quite astute. The time is coming. You must be there," the angel's voice called out.

"How will I know what to do?" I was terrified that I wouldn't be enough. That when the time came, I would fail.

"Things will unfold as they must, and you will react. Do not think about what you must do, for you will know when the time comes. Be brave, Izzy. The world needs you in these coming hours." Uriel seemed to believe in me, which made me all the more nervous.

"No pressure," I muttered.

"All of the pressure. If you fail, so fails the world." The jerky angel didn't seem to understand sarcasm at all.

"Sarcasm, Uriel. Surely you've heard of it?"

"I have." Uriel's voice began to fade, to be replaced by my aunt. "So, that's who that voice belongs to? Huh. Not at all who I would've guessed."

My aunt approached me, wrapping her arm around my shoulder and pulling me close. We stayed like that for what felt like a small eternity. Just breathing in the thick air, listening to the sounds of the swamp.

"You are a very brave girl, Izzy. Your mother would be very proud of you," Mona said quietly.

"I don't feel brave. I feel selfish. I keep thinking of everything I don't want to leave. I don't want to do this. I don't want to end my life. I don't want to die," I sobbed into her shoulder.

"Do we ever really die? No, we live on in those we love. You will never truly die, Izzy. What you do in the next hours will live on for an eternity." My aunt held me close, stroking my hair as my mother had done when I was young.

"But I won't be here. I won't be able to marry Kennan. I won't have children. I won't ever grow old. I won't ever reach thirty. There is so much that I will miss out on. I know I must do this. Ultimately, there is no other way. I just wish that I'd had more time." Every thought I'd kept to myself came rushing out. I confessed to my aunt what I'd been afraid to tell anyone else.

"None of us are ever guaranteed any amount of time. At least you know your day and you can face it bravely. All will not be lost, Izzy. You will be reunited with him one day," she promised.

"Do you know that for sure?"

"No, but I still hope," she replied honestly.

"We need to get moving. The longer I dwell on this, the more I feel the pull of the darkness. Everything in me is crying to submit." I pulled away, trying to get my thoughts under control.

"Then move we must. I will go gather everyone."

"Is it far?" I looked out into the swamp wondering just what sort of journey awaited us.

"No, not even a mile away. We will be there soon."

"Onward to destiny, then," I mumbled.

"Don't jump in the swamp while I'm gone!" My aunt shouted as she moved back into the house to gather everyone.

"Would you really jump?" Conall's voice sounded from my elbow.

"It's tempting."

"You're much more than I ever thought you would be, Izzy. I see now what my mother saw in you. I can't imagine how hard this is. I want you to know that I will be there for him, the same way he was there for me. He helped me out of the darkness when Cait died. I won't turn my back on him," Conall swore to me, and I could feel the binding of his words. He'd given me an oath.

I threw my arms around Conall, hugging him tightly. My pirate-patched friend. He knew exactly the right words to say.

"I hope that you and Sena find the sort of happiness that I had with Kennan. It would be a shame for that sort of love to just blink out of existence," I said between tears.

"Well, I don't think anyone will ever have the kind of love the two of you have, but I will try." Conall's voice seemed strained, as if he were holding back.

"We are ready," Eleanor said, causing me to jump away from Conall.

I quickly dried my eyes, erasing any of the emotions I'd been fighting. Kennan didn't need to see how scared I was. He needed me to be strong.

"Then let's go fight some demon." I moved in line behind one of the Order's Guardians on the boardwalk.

Chapter Twenty Seven

We moved through the swamp, unspeaking. The weight of what we were about to face settled down on us like a lead blanket. There was no escaping what would come. I just hoped that whatever we faced, I would be the only one to die.

Glancing back on the people walking behind me, I was surprised. We truly had an army marching into battle. There were at least twenty Guardians, all wearing new marks. Scattered amongst the behemoths were several Seers. I worried for them. Surely, they would be in danger, yet they still came. Eleanor and Mona walked along silently in the back of the group.

I wondered how much further it would be. Even with the runes being blocked, I still felt the pull on my energy. Just as the thought crossed my mind, the cypress trees parted to reveal the church I'd been seeing for months. My breath caught in my throat as I took it in. I knew, the end would be here today. I had no more days. Where Cait had been given an extra one, I would not.

"It's coming," I whispered.

"What is coming?" The Guardian ahead of me asked.

"The darkness. Don't you feel it?" I questioned as the dread multiplied inside of me.

"I don't feel anything." The unnamed Guardian supplied.

"We don't have much time!" I shouted to the group, breaking into a run, heading for the chapel.

I reached the edge of the cemetery and looked up to the thunderheads forming overhead. I knew that the battle raged on above me. I'd seen it more times than I could count. The end was here, my grand finale. I looked back to Kennan, who stood far off in the distance. "I love you," I whispered, hoping that the wind would carry my promise to him. My last chance to tell him how I truly felt. Time had run out.

A clap of thunder resounded, shaking the earth as it echoed repeatedly in the distance. The church shook, causing rubble to fall to the earth. I looked wide-eyed at the Guardians around me. As one, they whispered a word, something I'd never heard. Within a second, it happened, they began to transform. Some of them shifted into the great berserkers, some into wolves, some turned into creatures that seemed made of fire. All around me monsters reigned, only these monsters were there to help me. I couldn't lose heart now. The time had come.

The thunder clapped anew, ripping a tear in the fabric of the corporeal plane, revealing Sonneillon. He pulled his monstrous form through the tear, leaving it shredded in his wake. What other manner of beast would be able to make it through? Was he truly the only demon we would face? I stood, frozen to the ground as Emmanuel emerged behind him.

As the demon stepped through onto our plane the world seemed to quake. As if the very fabric of our world knew that the existence of such a being would be its demise. With each step Sonneillon took, the world became blackened. Nothing could live in the presence of such hatred, nothing could survive. The blackened earth spanned out beneath him, reminding me of the man I'd seen in my vision. Veins of darkness seemed to snake out from him as he stepped, seeking out a weakness that could be exploited. Just before the demon fully emerged, movement in the corner of my eye distracted me.

Aberto moved to intercept Emmanuel, engaging him in a battle that could have no winner. Emmanuel had been Aberto's brother, the way that Conall and Ian were Kennan's. I couldn't imagine them having to fight. Yet, I couldn't imagine them turning their backs on the world the way Emmanuel had.

"You will not succeed!" Aberto shouted, as his arms glowed brightly.

"I already have," Emmanuel choked out as Aberto threw him to the ground.

Aberto stood over him, a flaming sword in hand, "This is the end."

"I've done what I set out to do. Know this, I was not alone," Emmanuel choked out as Aberto plunged the flaming sword deep in his chest. With a flash of light, Emmanuel faded from my sight. I hoped that whatever judgment awaited him would be merciless.

Uriel had said he served a purpose. I still could not understand how bringing this demon to our plane could be of any good to anyone. Nothing made sense. An earth shattering roar shook me from my thoughts.

Sonneillon had made it through to our plane. He was so much more than I'd envisioned. He towered above us, his dark skin lit from within by some unholy flame. Bottomless pits of eternal flame shone from his face as he opened his maw to roar once more. An ancient fear, buried deep in my soul, awoke. Everything in me shouted for me to run, to hide from the demon, or submit to his will.

Hate churned within me, endless pain tore through my soul as the sound of a thousand men screaming filled my ears. The world was on fire, and I was powerless to calm the flames. The world would burn, of that I was sure. As the demon approached me, the darkness spread, snaking around me with relentless precision. I couldn't breathe as the weight of the lives that would be lost crashed in upon me. The screams erupted in my ears, a chorus of metal grating upon metal, an eternity of pain endured in the pits of hell.

"Izzy, move!" my aunt shouted as the beast lumbered towards me.

Conall jumped to intercept, tearing deeply into the demon's flesh. It did little to slow him down. I knew that I had to run, that I needed to avoid the demon. I remembered Uriel's words; that I would know what to do when the time came. He'd been wrong. I didn't know what I was supposed to do. I couldn't think straight as the fear coursed through my veins. How could I have been so naïve? I couldn't defeat this thing. I couldn't stop the darkness.

Frozen, I stood. The hate snaking about me, making it impossible for me to move. Visions flashed behind my eyes. Countless cities burning, black eyed men chasing down those that had yet to be taken. The world would end, the hate was too strong.

"Izzy!" Kennan's voice shouted, the only thing that could break through the fog. I began to run as the demon approached. I still didn't know what to do. I fought back the voices that screamed in my head. I had to focus.

Ten Guardians surrounded the demon, holding it back. They pressed it towards the tear between the planes. Pushing the beast back toward the opening, a glimmer of hope formed in my heart. If we could get it back through to the other plane, then it could end without any one dying. Just as my hope appeared, it was dashed to smithereens. In that instant, Sonneillon bellowed, a great flame rising from his gut as he threw the Guardians from him as though they were mere flies to be swatted away.

The Guardians tumbled to the sides, only to be replaced by more. The minutes passed slowly, an endless futile assault against the demon. Nothing could slow it down. Still, it moved in my direction. I waited for inspiration, to know what I should do. Nothing came. I was useless.

Fear snaked through me, freezing me once more. The visions multiplied, brother killing brother, destruction, pain, fear, hatred. Everything good in this world disappeared as the demon made its way slowly towards me. His advance was unhindered by the attacks of the Guardians. I swallowed back the fear, I had to move. I knew a sacrifice was required, but I knew not what I needed to do. I slowly moved one foot after another towards the beast. Praying that some sort of divine inspiration would make its way through the cacophony in my head.

"Izzy, NO!" I heard Kennan shout as the demon closed the distance between us. Kennan threw himself in the demon's path. Fighting it back as it moved closer towards me. The demon picked Kennan up as though he were a ragdoll and ripped him in two, throwing the pieces to the side as though he were nothing.

The world stopped as I stared in abject horror. Time seemed to slow as the pieces of the man I loved drifted to the ground, taking my heart with him. My entire world, all that mattered, dropped to the ground like so much refuse. Kennan wasn't supposed to die. Kennan was supposed to live, to survive this hell. I was the one that should've died. Never Kennan. Not him. Shock rooted me in place as the pieces finally hit the ground, speeding time up with their impact.

His body lay discarded on the ground as if he were nothing more than an obstacle in the demon's way. The man I loved couldn't be gone. This couldn't be real. He was supposed to *live*.

"He's not supposed to die," I whispered as tears began to stream down my face.

A high keening sound erupted from my lungs as I felt myself begin to pull apart. Pain ripped through my limbs as everything that had been taken from me rushed to the surface. I let the anger I'd been trying so hard to repress take me over. I didn't want to live. Not in a world where he did not exist. I let the blue fired engulf me as I moved toward the demon. The pain of the burning buoyed me as I resolved myself to end it all.

Sonneillon stopped in his tracks. His voice echoed in my head, shredding through my defenses. "You could not even protect the man you loved. How do you expect to defeat me? You were never strong enough."

I moved towards him as the fire grew inside of me, ripping away the person I'd been. I could feel the world slipping away as I moved toward the demon. He was right, I wasn't strong enough to protect Kennan. But I was strong enough to do this, to end everything so that he could never again return. As the pain grew to an apex, I reached out for the demon. I would never let him take someone away again. The loss I felt exploded within me, and I vowed to never let this happen again. I would end this.

Wrapping my arms around the demon, I could feel the world begin to fade.

Uriel's voice telling me that I would know what must be done.

Aberto's conversation with Kennan on the porch.
My childhood.
My family.
Everyone I loved.

Every step of my life had led me to this moment. Every single person I'd loved and lost, every battle I'd fought, every single second culminated in this moment.

I looked up into the demon's face and something I saw there shocked me. It wasn't the demon staring back, but someone entirely different. Emmanuel had been right. He wasn't alone. Staring back at me from the demon's eyes were the Council members. The people sworn to protect this world from the darkness had been behind it all along. Damali and Francesca smiled grimly from its eyes, promising that more would come.

Nothing was ever as it seemed in this broken world. I let go of it, of every bit of hate I felt. I let go, and I let the fire consume me.

A blinding light ripped out through the graveyard. I stood there holding out my arms as my mortal shell ripped apart, taking with it the demon. Nothing could exist inside of the fire, nothing could survive. My love, my anger, my hope, and my fear all joined together in that blinding fire. It would end, and with it went my life. Nothing made sense. Everything was lost.

The demon screamed out as it broke to pieces, shattering to onyx stones and melting into nothingness. I stared as the skin on my arms began to crack, the light blinding my eyes. My mortal shell shattered to bits as the demon broke, and so did I. I was no more.

The light ended. The sounds returned. Yet still, I stood. No longer me, but something else entirely.

I looked out upon the scorched field and fell to my knees. It was supposed to be over. I was supposed to go with him. I struggled to find air, trying to fight back the overwhelming fear that threatened to consume me. Had I failed? Was the demon going to come back? Understanding was beyond my grasp. Nothing made sense.

"Izzy?" I heard Aberto's voice, as if it were a thousand miles away. "Izzy, it is over. It is done."

"Then why am I still here?" I asked, angry at the heavens for being so cruel. How could I remain?

"You are no longer what you were." I could feel his approach, even without seeing it.

"Then what am I?"

"I don't know, Izzy. But we must leave this place. There are injured that must be tended to," Aberto pleaded.

"No one can bring him back," I whispered staring out at the scorched field.

"I know." Aberto's voice was calm as if he were trying to tame a wild animal.

"I can't leave him here." I muttered, crawling across the scorched earth towards his remains. Even torn to pieces, he was still my Kennan. The only person that had ever, or would ever, matter to me. He was my home, and now that home was gone forever. I moved slowly on all fours, choking back the sobs that threatened to pull me under.

"Izzy, don't." My aunt moved toward me, but I struck out with an invisible force, sending her falling back.

"Let me see him. I have to see him." I kept moving, ignoring the pressing silence, ignoring the fact that I had just Jedi-mind pushed my aunt, ignoring everything. "I have to see him," I whispered.

But when I did, it was all I could do to keep the contents of my stomach in place. This wasn't like the lab, he would not heal from this. Kennan lay in pieces, scattered over the battlefield. I cried out, hurrying to try and put his pieces back together. Maybe if I tried, maybe if I joined the halves back together, I could fix him. I could bring him back. Surely the heavens weren't this cruel. I sobbed, struggling to drag his halves back together, the only sound a deep keening inside of me. That's when Aberto came, that's when the darkness settled in.

Chapter Twenty Eight

The volume was turned up, the world came crashing back in, stealing away the blissful oblivion. Screams and shouts exchanged all around me. I struggled to open my eyes. I inhaled slowly trying to remember where I was, what had happened. Then reality came crashing back in on me. Kennan was gone. Forever.

"No. No. NO!" I shouted as a sob racked my body once more. Any numbness I might have felt during the battle had worn off. I shouldn't be alive. He'd stepped in to save me, when I could have saved him all along. It was my fault that he'd died. He could have been here with me. We could have had our one more day. We could've had so many more. I'd failed him.

"His death guided you to your destiny," my aunt's voice said, only I knew it was Uriel speaking.

"His death was a waste. I was the sacrifice. Me! Not him. Never him. Why was he taken?" Anger bellowed inside of me. I struggled to contain it, afraid that I may hurt someone if I let loose.

"His death was necessary. Without his death, you would have remained in your mortal shell, unable to send the demon back from whence it came," Uriel stated as if Kennan's death was no more than an item on a checklist to be marked off.

"But it doesn't matter, in the end. It will just come back. All of this death, this life, it is a pointless exercise in futility. You should have let me die." I stared at my aunt, seeing Uriel through her eyes. It was pointless, this life, this never ending cycle of war.

"You do not yet know? He has not told you?"

"Stop speaking in riddles. For once, just speak the truth," I shouted.

"You are no longer a mortal, Izzy." Uriel's words sank into me, awakening fears I'd been repressing. Somehow I knew this was coming.

"Then what am I?"

"You are what you are. I told you that there was a cost for the gifts that had been given. The cost is that you live to serve." Uriel seemed to think that I'd wanted this life, whatever it may be. I hadn't asked for these supposed "gifts."

"To what end? There is nothing to keep me here. Nothing to even tempt me to do as you ask. You could've found another way. Some way to intercede so that he could live." In a world without Kennan, there was nothing that I wanted to defend. Nothing that would even tempt me to do the bidding of the heavens. Everything had been taken from me, and now I was going to spend an eternity trapped.

"If he had lived, you would not have been able to defeat the darkness. If he had lived, even if you did somehow succeed, you would still have to watch him die. Life is not an eternal gift, Izzy. Life comes in brief bursts of light that are ended at a precise moment for a precise reason."

"What was the reason for his death? This is a war that has no end. His sacrifice was pointless. He could've lived. He could have thrived!" I spat.

"He died, so that countless others could live. He knew before the battle that this would be his fate. He faced it with honor. Do not do him the disservice of taking that away." Uriel's words sank into me, throwing my thoughts back to the memory of Aberto and Kennan talking.

"He didn't know. He thought I would die. He didn't know." I shook my head, fighting back the tears. Nothing made sense. I wondered if it ever would again.

"Izzy, he did know." Aberto's voice pulled my attention away from my aunt.

"What do you know, Aberto? What aren't you telling me?" I begged.

"I saw it, from the day I tattooed your back, I knew what would come."

I got up from where I lay, beating against him. Raging against the man that was supposed to protect me. The man that had sworn he loved me, yet he let Kennan die. Had he done it for selfish reasons? Had he hoped that this end may turn me towards him in my mourning?

"How could you let him die? You swore to protect me. You swore to keep me safe. How can I ever be safe again if he isn't here?" I raged against him, refusing to suppress anything.

"I had no other course of action." Aberto grabbed my arms pinning them to his chest. "Do you not think that this has weighed on me every day? Do you not know how many times I've longed to warn you? The most I was permitted to do was tell him. He took it honorably, he lived his last days with you knowing that they would soon end. Izzy, he died so that you may live."

"But I'm not alive, not really. Am I?" It was a waste, his death. It had done nothing to save me. I was broken.

"You exist between planes." Aberto's soft voice broke through anger.

"So you made me like you." I slid to my knees, wishing for the oblivion of the darkness. I wanted to surround myself in it.

"I had no idea when I breathed my soul into you that this would be the consequence."

"But you said you saw!" I shouted, growing more hysterical by the moment. "You said that you saw him die. Which means that you must've seen me."

"I saw you die as well. Today. But everything changed when you marked the Seers. You weren't meant to die then. Not back there. Since then, since I did everything I could to keep you alive, I have been unable to see your future clearly."

"Better I had died that day than live a thousand more days without him. You should have let me go." I curled in on myself, trying to hold what remained of me together.

"And where would the world be now if I had, Izzy?"

"Fuck the world, Aberto. I don't give a damn about this wretched place. The only person I could depend on, my home, my anchor is gone. None of this matters to me anymore." I pulled myself to stand once more, my anger buoying me. I waved my hands around me as people began to close in.

"Izzy?" My aunt hesitated, afraid to come much closer. "Izzy, I don't know what to say."

"Make it worth it. Make his death worth your lives, because otherwise, I will summon the damn demon back myself." As I looked out on the people I'd once cared for a knot began to form. I needed to get away. I needed to escape all of their expectant eyes. I couldn't breathe as their hopes and fears crashed in on me simultaneously. I had to go. I had to leave.

"Izzy, calm yourself," Aberto admonished.

I rose to my feet, every bit of anger fueling me as I struck him across his face.

"Don't you dare tell me to calm myself! Kennan just *died*. Not even an hour ago. So don't for one moment think that I will be calm. Not now, not tomorrow, not even the next day. I will never be her again. The sooner you all recognize that, the better. I'm done with this whole 'Izzy is the savior of the world' bullshit. I'm done being the one to lose everything and everyone I love just for the sake of everyone else. You all wanted to know when I would finally snap? Well, it just happened. I'm done, Aberto." I felt myself waiver out of existence.

I could escape. I could flee this plane altogether. Aberto had. He'd spent hundreds of years in the fog, just drifting. Anything would be better than this; these eyes staring at me. The people that supposedly cared for me, yet did nothing to keep Kennan alive. If I really wanted to face the truth, Kennan was dead because I didn't act quickly enough. I'd let my fear paralyze me, and because of that, I'd paid the price.

I looked up at Aberto. He saw it, I knew he did. There was no mistaking my intent. I just hoped that now that I was whatever I was, I could hide from him in the dreaming. I didn't want to be found. I wanted to disappear. I wanted to be swept away from this wretched place.

"Izzy, don't!" Aberto shouted as I slipped between planes straight into the comforting fog of the dreaming. Sweet oblivion.

Chapter Twenty Nine

Wading through the fog, I sought out something, anything that may bring me release. Some form of comfort to relieve the pain that had opened up in my chest. My soul ached as though it had been torn right alongside Kennan. Even when my parents had died, I didn't feel this gaping chasm inside of me. I ran, panicked, through the fog, afraid that if I settled for too long in one place the image of Kennan being torn to pieces would play itself out once more.

I ran for what seemed an eternity, never finding any refuge. Then I thought of it, the last place we'd been normal together. Our home. I wanted to go home. I needed to go home, to see Kennan's comfy chair and the stupid dead garden that I could never quite get to grow. The last place we'd been able to just be together beckoned me, calling me into its bosom.

I ripped through the dreaming, the same way Aberto had drug me a thousand times. I pulled myself out with a snap, landing in the middle of my old living room. The house settled around me, making noises as if to invite me home. I walked passed Kennan's old chair, letting my fingers trail across the smooth leather, and ultimately lowering myself into the chair to bask in his scent. My hands ran up and down the arms of the chair of their own accord, as if wishing on some genie lamp. If only that could work. If only I had some hope of ever seeing him again.

Quickly, I moved away from his smell. This was meant to be a refuge, yet all it was turning out to be was an entombment. An empty reminder of a life that was no more. A mausoleum for a future that could never exist. Shaking my thoughts away, my feet carried me up the stairs to our room. That's when I realized, I never should have come.

As I turned the corner into our room, I came face to face with the cruelest reminder of all that the life I'd wanted, the life we'd hoped to share, would never be. There, hanging on the wardrobe, was my wedding dress. I'd gotten it just days before we'd been called to the Council. So much had happened, so much had changed. How had I so readily given up on this life with him? He'd been right all along. I'd chosen wrong. I walked to the dress, running my hands over the soft folds of the white fabric.

White fabric. It ought to have been red for all the blood on my hands. I ripped the mockery of happiness that could never be from the hanger, throwing it to the ground. I wanted to tear the stupid thing apart, stitch by stitch, so that it resembled me. Shattered, scattered remains of something that could've been beautiful. The reminder of a promised life of love was too much.

Falling to the floor, I let myself get lost in the comfort of what our future might have been. I could see children running through the halls, echoes of laughter bouncing all around. A garden that somehow actually managed to grow was just outside of the open windows. Kennan chased our kids down the stairs and outside, pretending to be a monster as they giggled and squealed with delight. A million scenarios of ordinary days played out before my eyes, only they were extraordinary. Every breath that would be left untaken, every heartbeat left to silence, every moment and every second played out before me. The life I could have had, if I'd just chosen correctly.

Isadora had told me once that I would've been happy, that I would lead my life in blissful glee with my family. Yet, I'd thought my place was there, helping with the Seers. What did I have to show for it? I'd lost so much. Kennan, my parents, even myself. I was left with nothing and it was all because I'd made the wrong decision.

But now it was too late. I'd made my bed and now I'd have to pay the consequences. Kennan's death was on my hands. The world had lost something beautiful because I'd given everything to fight an unwinnable battle.

"Why can't I just die?" I screamed out to the heavens as a sob wracked my body. I wanted to fade away, to be with him. At least then, this might have all been worth the price.

"You must pay for the gifts you were given." A voice whispered through the air.

"I never asked for this!" I shouted, trying to keep myself together.

"Yet you were given, none the less. Now, you must endure the cost of what was given to you." Uriel's voice rang out.

"How long must I endure this? How long must I journey between planes, never finding refuge? This seems a worse hell than any the demon might have brought forth."

"Yours is a life of wonder, Izzy. You will not die." Uriel came into view, standing over me a flaming visage.

"I will never see an end," I whispered, afraid.

"All things see an end. Perhaps when this world is no more, you too shall be free."

"Why must I pay for something that I never asked for?" I longed for some sort of answer, something that would help to make sense of it all.

"You are not the only one paying for Aberto's actions," Uriel promised, doing nothing to ease my pain.

"So, you are telling me that me being like this is some form of demented punishment for him?"

"All actions have consequences, Izzy," Uriel breathed, as if I'd become a nuisance.

"Fuck you and your consequences!" I yelled, ripping myself from the house and back into the dreaming. I'd had enough. I could see why people would turn against the world. I now understood why Aberto had disappeared for so long. It had all been for nothing. Every gain, every loss, every lesson learned was all for naught.

As I drifted into the fog to be lost, one thought crossed my mind. The Council members. I'd seen them, in the demon's eyes. They'd been behind it the whole time, using Emmanuel as some sort of puppet to do their bidding. If I had anything left in me, I would care. Now, after I'd given everything I had, it meant nothing. Let the world burn. Let man turn against man. It was an endless, unwinnable battle. Pointless.

I breathed a goodbye to the world I'd known. I was Izzy Boone no more, that girl died right alongside Kennan on the battlefield. Every part of me that had loved, that had lost, everything that made me who I'd been, was gone. My life should have ended. I should have fallen, and so fall I would into the deepest chasm the dreaming had to offer. I would wait there for the end of time. I was no more.

"Hello, oblivion," I whispered, falling back into the endless swirling vortex of the dreaming. As the darkness closed in, I was finally greeted with some respite. Numbness cascaded over me as I sought out the darkest corner the dreaming had to offer.

Chapter Thirty

Molly

"What do you mean he's dead? How in the hell did you people let that happen?" I shouted into the phone. I knew we should've gone with them to the Order. I'd been too concerned with Ian's delicate situation and I hadn't been there for my friends when they needed me the most. "Where's Izzy? What happened?"

"I will come and explain everything." Aberto's voice sounded drawn on the other end. Like I gave a rat's ass how he felt. He'd been the one that got Izzy caught up in this whole mess to begin with. If it hadn't been for him tampering with the laws of humanity, Izzy would still be safe at the Council with their help instead of with the crazy witchdoctors in the swamp.

"Well, come on then. Poof yourself here." I slammed the phone shut, fighting the urge to throw it against the wall. Too much had happened over the past year.

"Is it true?" Ian asked from my side. His voice strained, barely masking the tears that threatened to burst the dam at any moment.

"Kennan's gone. Aberto's on his way to tell us what happened now," I said with ruthless efficiency. I couldn't let my emotions get the best of me. I had to stay focused until I knew what was really going on.

"I should've been there." Ian got up from the couch and began to pace. "I should've manned up and gone with my brother. He's always had my back and the one time he needs me, I flake out."

"What could you have done? You being there wouldn't have changed a durn thing and you know it. Kennan knew what it meant for you to go back there, to the Order. He wouldn't have asked that of you." I swore under my breath. If there was one thing I'd learned about Ian over the past year, it was that he held onto stuff tightly and for immeasurable amounts of time. I knew he'd never forgive himself for not being there.

"It should have been me, not him," Ian choked out.

I rose from my seat, reaching up on the tiptoes to slap him across his stupid dense face. "Don't you dare ever say anything that dumb again, do you understand me?"

Ian stared down at me, shocked for a moment, before pulling me close to his chest. Things had not been easy for us. We'd been playing the hot then cold game for longer than I could remember, but lately, with the world falling apart, things had changed. With my mom, the traitorous bitch, and his sketchy past, we'd found some sort of bridge. Plus, he'd finally started dressing in a socially acceptable manner. That one still surprised me.

"I just can't believe he's gone. Izzy! Where is she?" Ian pulled back, concern etched across his face setting off my lingering handprint nicely.

"Aberto is coming. He said he would explain." I just hoped he would get there quickly.

"Well, he needs to hurry it up and get here. I need to know, Molly. I have to know what happened to him." Ian's voice threatened to break.

"He's coming, just try and stay calm. Freaking out isn't going to bring him back. Right now we need to try and keep ourselves together and find out what in the hell is going on first." I was ever the sensible one in our duo. Really, I'd never had the luxury of allowing my emotions to come out and play. I'd always had to repress everything in order to maintain the status quo.

Just like that Aberto appeared in the room. Instead of the normal withdrawn, cocky expression he tended to wear, there was fear. He looked broken, still covered in the blood from the battle.

"What's happened?" Ian rushed toward Aberto.

"They're gone." Aberto swayed before falling to his knees. "I didn't protect her."

"You're not making any sense. Tell us what's happened!" I yelled. Hoping to pull him out of his misery long enough to find out what had transpired.

"The battle, I knew he would die. I've always known. I told him, and he did what I'd seen him do over and over. He stepped in when Izzy could not move. His death drew her out and then, something happened. I'm not sure. There was a blinding blue light that burned. It ripped through the surroundings, scorching everything in its path. She clung to the demon as the blue light ripped through them both. She was gone."

"You said she didn't die. What do you mean she's gone?" I was getting ready to haul off and slap Aberto. It seemed to be a slapping sort of day. If he didn't start making some sense I was gonna lose my shit.

"She was gone, but as the light faded, she reappeared. She stood in the center of the scorched field, changed. She isn't mortal now. She's something different, and it is my fault."

"What happened? You aren't telling us anything!" I shouted, hoping to pull Aberto from his thoughts.

"Kennan, he stepped in to save Izzy and the demon ripped him to pieces as if he were made of mere parchment. Sonneillon threw him to the side like refuse. Something in her changed. She broke when she saw him die. After the demon was gone, she tried to piece Kennan back together. I had to make her sleep. When she finally awoke back at the Order, she was gone. She isn't Izzy any longer. She cares not what becomes of this world. I've taken everything from her, and given her nothing but an accursed existence in return."

"Where is she?" Ian wrapped a hand in Aberto's shirt, pulling him to his feet.

"I know not." Aberto had been broken right along with Izzy. Nothing would ever be the same again if we didn't find her and bring her home.

"Right, well then, we need to have a talk, you and me," I said to Ian. "And you, stop being a sad sack of suckage and go find our girl. I don't care how long it takes you. Something isn't right, and if Izzy needs help, then we are going to help her. She has lost everything to this world, we can't let her spend the rest of her eternity alone. So go, get moving, find her!" I shooed Aberto, hoping to scoot him off to the plane of the dreaming.

"I do not know where to find her." Aberto seemed wholly broken.

"You know her. Probably better than anyone else does. Try to think like her, where she might go, who she might reach out to. Get the Old Man gang together if you have to, but you find her. Don't come back until you've at least figured out where she might be. She needs you now, more than ever. She might not know it yet, but it is true. Stop standing here getting your sad all over the place and go." I gave his shoulder a nudge causing him to nod in ascent.

As he faded from the room I turned my attention toward Ian. The next bit wasn't going to be easy.

"I know," he said before I could even get the words out of my mouth.

"You know what?" I asked, annoyed at his tone.

"We have to go to the Order. Just so you know, things are different there," Ian sighed, running a hand over his head.

"Ian, I grew up inside of the Corporation, my mother is completely psychotic, and I've just been bounced from the Council. I am in no position to judge. Besides, I've been in your closet. That much plaid could *not* have come from anywhere normal," I smiled, hoping to pull Ian from his misery.

"How are you so upbeat right now? Kennan's dead and Izzy is missing." Ian seemed perplexed by my attitude. I'd be the first to admit, optimism wasn't typically my jig.

"I'm channeling Izzy, okay? She wouldn't let the circumstances stop her, and neither will I. Not until we get her back and she can take over being Suzie Optimist again. Until then, I'm going to keep plowing ahead. If I stop and let the sadness take me down I won't be any good to her. I'm not letting that girl down! Do you understand me?" I leveled Ian with a steady, unrelenting gaze. It was time we got cracking.

"Okay, fine, but I need to make some calls before I am even able to return. This isn't going to be as easy as you hope," Ian sighed, pulling out his phone.

"We have to try. If there is anything we can do to find her, we have to. She would do it for us." I paused for a moment, letting reality sink in. Izzy was gone. Well and truly gone from this world. She'd been like the sister I'd never wanted, but was super happy to have. I couldn't lose her, not after everything we'd been through. It wasn't fair for it to end this way. It couldn't end like this, with her gone and Kennan dead. If I had any say in the matter, it wouldn't. Damn it.

Chapter Thirty One

Molly

Running up to my room to throw a bag together, I tried to formulate a plan. Sure we should go to the Order to be with everyone, but what then? I had a terrible feeling about what was going on. It felt unresolved, like this wasn't the end of the story. Prophecy or no prophecy, something was off. Shaking it off, I ran into what used to be Izzy's room to put the last touches on my bounce bag. I hadn't gotten out of the habit of keeping one packed, and the last few months had taught me more than anything that it was a worthwhile practice.

"Molly, someone wishes to speak to you." Ian held his phone out to me as he stood in the doorway. He'd started respecting the whole "my space" rule after the hair dye incident. I think the ten deadbolts I'd installed also had something to do with it.

"Who?" I questioned, unsure of who might be calling me.

"Just take it, please." Ian tossed the phone towards me. Not waiting to see if I would catch it.

"Hello?" I was hesitant.

"Oh good, Molly, thank goodness." Eleanor's voice came from the receiver.

"We're coming your way. Ian has some reservations that he won't be allowed back. So, tell the Order that they can shove it if they think we are staying away at a time like this." I plowed ahead, still channeling Izzy.

"Molly, I presume?" an entirely new voice said.

"Yes, and you are?" I asked, probably more abruptly than was necessary. I just didn't want to play the whole mask of mystery game that Seers seemed so prone to like to play.

"I'm Mona, Izzy's aunt and the Grand Seer of the Order. Tell our Ian he is welcome back anytime he would like. There is much that we would like to discuss with him upon his return. Have no fears, you will both be welcome here. But I fear you must hurry. Things are moving more quickly than we had hoped."

"Aunt? Izzy has an aunt?" Okay, so I probably should have gotten more out of all of that, but I'd thought Izzy had no family left. I thought about her and how she must've reacted to that news. Then it dawned on me, Ian had known all along.

"Yes, dear. You are losing sight of what is important. We are going to send the helicopter to retrieve you. Please be at the airfield as quickly as possible. See you both soon." Without so much as a goodbye, she hung up.

"She has an aunt?" I turned toward Ian, shocked.

"Yes. Before you start shrieking at me, let me explain, woman." Ian held up his hands in placation.

"I don't shriek. I'm shrill." I narrowed my eyes up at him.

"That is debatable." Ian ran a hand over his surprisingly tame hair. "When a person leaves the Order they are not permitted to speak of it, or the people within. It is part of the oath you take upon separation. Even had I wanted to tell her, it wouldn't have done any good. She'd chosen to lead the Council."

"But that is like taking a choice away from her, Ian. Don't you see that? She had a right to know." I threw a pair of balled up socks at him. "Go get packed. We have a chopper to catch."

"A chopper?" Ian asked with a raised brow.

"You know what I mean. We have to be down there within the hour. So hustle, mister. Stop lollygagging. I want to find Izzy and figure out what really happened back there. Aberto's half-assed attempts at explaining it aren't working for me."

"Alright, I'm moving." Ian paused before moving on. "She'll be okay, you know? She's tougher than she thinks."

"Yeah, but right now she thinks she is alone, Ian." I had to choke down a sob as I thought of Izzy out there by herself dealing with everything that had happened.

"We'll find her," Ian promised.

"Not if you don't go pack, we won't," I admonished.

"I'm going, stop nagging me, woman."

I plopped down on my bed thinking of Izzy, of what she must be going through right this moment. It was all too much. To feel so alone. I couldn't imagine life without Ian, not that I'd admit that to him. Izzy and Kennan, they were what little girls dreamed about when they were young. Their love was supposed to end in a happily ever after. Instead it just ended, abruptly.

"Alright, I'm ready." Ian pulled my bag from my hands as I headed to the door.

******

We rode to the airport in relative silence. I knew this wouldn't be an easy trip for Ian. After all, he hadn't been back to the Order in hundreds of years. Ian was a good man, though, and I knew without a doubt he would do whatever it took to bring Izzy back. If not for my sake, then for his friend's. Kennan had taken him in when he left the Order with no judgments. He'd tolerated him throughout the years, even with his horrible fashion sense. There was nothing Ian wouldn't do for Kennan. Even if that meant interceding on Izzy's behalf.

"What are you thinking?" Ian's voice pulled me from my thoughts.

"I'm thinking that it isn't fair. None of this." I stared out the window, trying to come to terms with all that had transpired.

"Things seldom are in our world." Ian reached out to lace his fingers with mine, giving me a comfort I hadn't known I needed.

"I don't think any of us understood what was at stake. She walked in there thinking that she would be the only one to die. She faced it, and now she is just gone. She was supposed to be freed from this world and now what? Is she stuck forever? She won't ever see him again, Ian."

"I know, Molly. I know." Ian pulled me against his body. I let his strength buoy me. I couldn't falter. I had to keep channeling the fearless Izzy. She'd stop at nothing to keep her friends safe.

We approached the airfield and paid the cab driver. Getting out, I noticed the same pilot that had flown us from the Council was here now.

"Ian," the pilot said.

"Bruce. Thanks for meeting us here, brother." Ian embraced him.

"It is a hard time for us all. We need you now more than ever," Bruce replied.

"Let's get going." Ian nodded toward the helicopter.

I settled into my seat, strapping on the many harnesses. I wasn't taking any chances. Planes were one thing, but helicopters? Well, let's just say that my last flight had about sent me into conniptions. I tried to think of anything else as the helicopter began to take off. I allowed Ian and Bruce's conversation from the front take my mind away from where I was. Maybe if I closed my eyes and did some of the breathing exercises I'd learned from Izzy's left behind yoga dvd's, I could relax.

I lay my head against the head rest, taking in deep, cleansing breaths and slowly letting them back out. I could do this, I could relax. Just as I finally found my focus, I heard it, the sobbing. I knew I needed to go, but I couldn't find where it was. That was the worst part about my ever developing abilities, I couldn't seem to hone them. My brain was a conduit for other Seers' thoughts, emotions, and visions. It was disorienting and sickening simultaneously.

"Who's there?" I called out in my mind.

"The darkness will still come." The sobbing continued.

I couldn't find it. Finally, I gave up and threw myself into the dreaming. At least then I could get a better grasp on everything.

"Where are you?"

"It was supposed to end. Why didn't it end?" the voice cried out.

"Who are you?" I asked again, certain that this time, maybe they would answer. Sometimes, I should really be careful what I wished for though. Out of the fog a figure emerged and I suddenly knew exactly what Izzy must've felt like talking to Ren.

Standing before me was a figure with scorched, blackened skin and blood running from every orifice. It was the most horrifying sight my eyes had ever beheld and I longed to look away, to hide my face. Instead, I pressed on.

"Who are you?"

"I am you." I looked more closely at the figure, trying to tell myself that it couldn't be true. This

218

scorched and tortured figure couldn't be me. Then I saw my eyes, staring back at me.

"But how?"

"The darkness is coming."

The figure reached out and pushed me from the dreaming.

Gulping for air, I opened my eyes. It wasn't over. Even if the demon was gone, something was still coming. Nothing was ever easy.

The End

Epilogue
Izzy

"The darkness shall fall," the shadows whispered. I longed to ignore them, to drift in the oblivion of the dreaming. I'd found comfort there for I wasn't sure how long. I really didn't care, to be honest. I wanted the days to pass. I wanted the days to end. There was nothing to tempt me. Nothing to make me long to live.

The thought of Molly and Ian skirted through my mind for a moment before skittering away from my disregard. They had each other. They could be happy. Then came the thought of my aunt. She'd lived her whole life without me, she didn't need me either. Person after person ran through my mind like some sort of torture. The memories weren't enough to mend the gaping chasm left by Kennan.

Kennan, his memories made every other memory worth the torture. His smile, his laugh, and the way his hands would brush the hair from my face before he'd kiss me. Each moment I relived reopened the wound, assuring that I would never be whole again. Kennan had been so much more to me than even I had known. By the time I'd figured it out, it had been too late.

"The darkness shall fall," the shadows whispered again. The whispers came from I knew not where. I did my best to ignore them but they were persistent bastards. Why couldn't I float in the darkness, alone, in peace? Hadn't I given enough?

"The war rages on," the shadows promised.

"Yeah, the damned war never ends. That's not news to me!" I shouted back.

"Act now or all will be lost."

"I've heard that before," I mumbled, shaking off the whispers and jumping back on memory lane.

Kennan walked up behind me at the sink in our farmhouse, kissing my shoulder, pulling me back against his body. I knew what he wanted, and I could never deny him. I needed him the way I needed air.

"Weep not the lost, for more shall fall," the shadows whispered.

"I'm trying to exist in solitary confinement here. Move along," I grumbled, trying to get my mind back where it had been.

"If you do not act, all will be lost."

"The darkness shall fall."

"The war rages on."

"Act now or all will be lost."

"More shall fall."

The whispers kept going and going, repeating the same things over and over again. I was going mad. That had to be it. Madness would be better than sanity at this point. At least in madness, I might be able to forget.

"The darkness will fall."

"Oh my GOD! Can you not say anything else?" Stupid whispers. Why couldn't they leave me alone?

"The war rages on."

"Heard that one already," I grumbled.

"You know not what you must do."

"Well at least that one is a new one."

"You must not linger here, do not make my death mean nothing." Kennan's voice broke through the others.

"Kennan?" I looked around me, trying to find him. He was there, somehow. Or was it another cruel trick that pulled at my mind?

"The darkness will fall."

"Kennan!"

"Linger not, for I am with you always." Kennan's voice faded as his face flashed before my eyes. What a cruel, cruel joke for my mind to play on me.

"Kennan, don't leave me again. Please stay." But I knew he was gone, or the phantom of him was.

"The war rages on."

"Oh for the love of all that is holy, please just stop."

"We can never stop."

"Oh, so now you are answering me?" I looked around me into the inky darkness and saw flashes of movement. "Who's there?"

As one, figures began emerging from the fog. Each one more disfigured than the last. Their skin a charred black I'd seen only days, or had it been months, before. I looked upon them in horror. These ghosts sent to taunt me, to mock what I'd given.

"The darkness is coming. The darkness will fall," a female voice promised. I looked more closely at her. I had a strange feeling that I somehow knew her, and as she raised her blood caked eyes to mine, I knew exactly who she was. Molly.

I swung around to look at everyone standing there. The source of the whispers. Ian muttered, "The war rages on," while Conall circled around muttering the same thing over and over again. Sena stepped forward, warning that I knew what I must do. They circled about me like sharks, waiting to take down their prey, moving ever closer. I longed to move, to run, but I'd trapped myself here. I was lost in the dreaming, there was no escape from them.

"The darkness will fall, and you are the bringer," my aunt lunged for me, wrapping her hand around my throat. Cutting off any objection I may have made.

"Act now, Izzy, or all will be for naught." Just like that they disappeared.

Had I been here before? I couldn't remember. Had I seen them, really, or were they just another manifestation of my mind?

I shook it all away, and returned to floating, lost in the dreaming. Far from everyone except the memories of Kennan.

Made in the USA
Lexington, KY
26 June 2014